FAMILY TREE

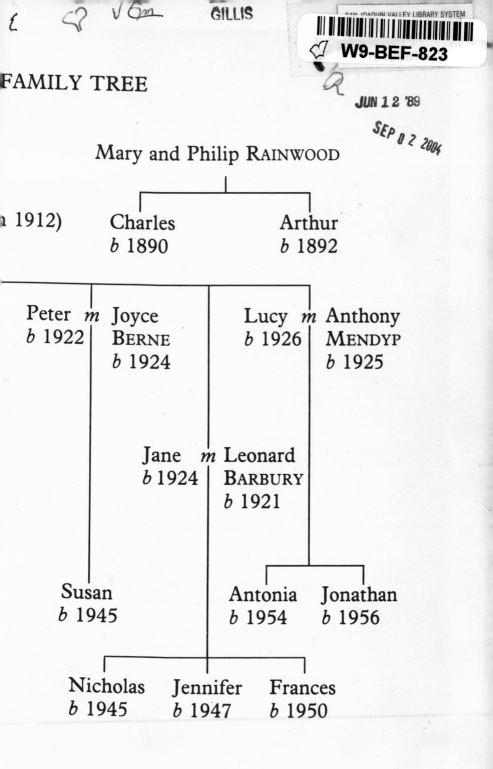

Mary and Philip RAINWOOD

1912)   Charles   Arthur
b 1890   *b* 1892

Peter *m* Joyce   Lucy *m* Anthony
b 1922   BERNE   *b* 1926   MENDYP
      b 1924   *b* 1925

Jane *m* Leonard
b 1924   BARBURY
     b 1921

Susan   Antonia   Jonathan
b 1945   *b* 1954   *b* 1956

Nicholas   Jennifer   Frances
b 1945   *b* 1947   *b* 1950

I've travelled the world twice over,
Met the famous: saints and sinners,
Poets and artists, kings and queens,
Old stars and hopeful beginners,
I've been where no-one's been before,
Learned secrets from writers and cooks
All with one library ticket
To the wonderful world of books.

THE STEPDAUGHTER

Mirabel Rainwood was a born matriarch and it was her influence which kept the family together. Living nearby, the numerous members of all generations met for Mirabel's traditional tea at Bredon Lodge on the first Saturday of every month. Bridget, "the stepdaughter," had always remained on the fringe of the family until Felix Parvey's engagement to Susan Rainwood. The Rainwoods had expected the boy-and-girl friendship between Felix and Bridget to end in marriage, and their concern for her proved to be a mixed blessing.

Books by Iris Bromige in the
Ulverscroft Large Print Series:

IRIS BROMIGE

THE STEPDAUGHTER

Complete and Unabridged

ULVERSCROFT
Leicester

First printed 1966

First Large Print Edition
published May 1980
by arrangement with
Hodder & Stoughton Ltd.
London

British Library CIP Data

Bromige, Iris
    The stepdaughter.—Large print ed.
    (Ulverscroft large print series: romance)
    I. Title
    823'.9'1F   PR6052.R572S/

    ISBN 0-7089-0452-1

Published by
F. A. Thorpe (Publishing) Ltd.
Anstey, Leicestershire
Printed in England

1

BIRTHDAY OF AN OLD LADY

MIRABEL RAINWOOD sat at her bureau in the drawing-room writing in her diary while the snow fell steadily past the window, muffling the garden with its gentle, inexorable cover. The only sounds in the room were the ticking of the old-fashioned ormolu clock on the mantelpiece, the silky flutter of the flames on the hearth beneath, and the faint scratch of the steel nib across the paper.

My birthday today. I am seventy-two. We are not having any celebration as Charles is in bed with a severe attack of lumbago, and the weather is too bad to expect the children to travel here. Pamela came this morning with a present from them all—a Georgian silver fruit stand. A beautiful piece. Very extravagant of them.

Pleased to have birthday cards from all ten grandchildren and Bridget.

1

A little worried by the talk linking Susan with Felix Parvey. Pamela hinted that an engagement was probable. I can't believe it. Bridget and Felix have been inseparable for so many years. I expect it is just family gossip based on very little.

She broke off as she heard voices in the hall, and a warm smile softened the austerity of her face when a tall, broad-shouldered man came into the room.

"Robert, my dear boy! What a pleasant surprise! I thought you were in Wales."

"I left early this morning. As I was passing so close, and it's your birthday, I had to look in. Many happy returns of the day, Grandma," he said, kissing the cheek she proffered.

"Thank you, dear. And thank you, too, for the lovely flowers that came this morning. You see them around you. Spring flowers on a snowy January day are so good for the morale. Now come and have a warm by the fire. Gwen will be bringing tea soon. She was pleased to see you, I know."

"Welcomed me like a long-lost son. Told me that Grandpa was in bed with lumbago.

You, I am glad to see, look as invincible as ever."

"And you look tired, my dear. Were the roads very bad?"

"Not the main roads. These side lanes are a bit tricky. This is good," he added, leaning back in the armchair and stretching his long legs to the fire. "I've interrupted your writing, I'm afraid."

"And a very happy interruption, too. My diary can wait," said Mirabel, who had closed it and put it away in the drawer as soon as he came into the room, but not before he had noted it.

"They would make interesting reading, those diaries of yours, Grandma. They must cover a period of great social change. When did you first start keeping a diary?"

"When I was fifteen, King Edward was on the throne, Asquith was Prime Minister and my first entry is an enthusiastic description of my first visit to a London theatre to see Beerbohm Tree in Julius Caesar."

"Halcyon days until the 1914 war broke it all up. And you've kept it up all these years?"

"Yes. The entries for some years are a little thin, but the record of our family affairs is a fairly complete one."

"I guess it would often prove salutary reading," said Robert with a wry smile.

"I have always found it helpful to clarify my feelings by writing. My entries have had to be brief. That kind of discipline helps to keep woolly-mindedness at bay."

"I doubt if your mind was ever woolly, Grandma."

Gwen came in then with the tea-trolley, and Robert Rainwood watched his grandmother pour out tea from the silver teapot with an expression of amused affection on his face.

"And are Rainwood and Trawler busy?" she asked.

"Very. We've taken on a new articled clerk who seems a promising lad."

"And how is old Mr. Trawler?"

"Not very well, I'm afraid. He'll definitely retire at the end of the summer. He would have retired before, of course, if things had been different. I'm grateful to him for staying on these two years."

"Will you take on another partner?"

"I doubt it."

"You ought to marry, Robert, and have sons to carry on."

"There would be no guarantee that they

4

would want to be solicitors, Grandma."

"Your father might have said the same, but you chose his profession."

"Well, I'm content with my bachelor state and not inclined to change it for the sake of offspring."

"I think it's a pity."

"If you have a yen for great-grandchildren, Grandma, take comfort from the fact that one of your grandchildren, at least, has matrimony in mind. I suppose you've heard about young Susan?"

"Only rumours. Is it true, Robert?"

"Yes. Susan let me into the secret before I left for Wales. She said they were going to announce it this weekend. What's the matter? Don't you approve of Felix Parvey?"

"I'd assumed it would be Bridget he would marry."

"Really?"

"Yes. Bridget told me in the autumn that there was an understanding between them but that Felix wouldn't make it official until he'd taken over the editorship of the magazine, which he expected to do shortly."

Robert whistled, then said:

"Well, well. This will set the family humming. I knew that Bridget and Felix had been friends, of course, but I assumed that it was just a boy and girl affair that had faded out with time. Felix took over the editorship at Christmas, so Susan told me. Have you seen Bridget lately?"

"On Christmas morning, when she slipped in with a present. She seemed happy enough then."

"Well, perhaps they both had second thoughts," said Robert cheerfully, helping himself to another piece of buttered toast.

"Susan's an attractive girl and has always known what she wanted. How do you find her in the office, Robert?"

"Very efficient, I believe. She works on Trawler's side and I haven't had much to do with her in a business capacity. Don't believe in working with relations, even a cousin as pretty and competent as Susan. But she graduated from the typists' room to being Miss Gordon's assistant in a very short time, and took her place most adequately while she was away on holiday. Now, of course, just as she's fully trained and really useful, she'll be leaving us. From the way she spoke, the engagement will be a short one. I think she aims at a spring wedding. I'm surprised that you don't know about it. You, the matriarch. Are they afraid to tell you?"

He was the only member of the Rainwood family who ever dared to tease her, and she shook her head at him to indicate that, although he was privileged, she did not really approve.

"I expect they will be in touch with me today. Don't repeat what I've told you about Felix and Bridget. It was told me in confidence, and I've never mentioned it to anybody until today, but I know I can rely on your discretion. Everybody knows that they've been close friends for years, but it will be better to behave as though no more than friendship has ever been involved."

"And has it? Aren't you assuming too much, perhaps? Girls can have romantic fancies about understandings that don't really go deep."

"I think it does go deep with Bridget. Her circumstances are different from most other girls. She's led a rather solitary life, at home with her father. Her friendship with Felix has filled her life, brought it the only warmth it has. She's on my conscience, you know, Robert. Your Uncle Owen's unsociability and coolness towards the family has tended to cut Bridget off, too. She's always hovered on the fringe of the family and I feel I should have done more to draw her in, no matter what her father felt."

"Her stepfather, you mean."

"Yes. That's been part of the trouble, perhaps. Coupled with your Uncle Owen's attitude, it's made the family behave as though Bridget was of little concern to them."

"But you've always kept an eye on her, and she's not exactly a child any longer. How old is she? Early twenties, I suppose."

"Twenty-three. She's a warm-hearted girl, and her home life has been such a cold one since her mother died. Felix made up for a lot, though, and helped her with her writing. She's doing quite well, in a modest way, with her journalism. She does a weekly article for The Monitor, you know, and Felix gives her other assignments as well. But I think it would have been better for her if she had taken a full-time job on a magazine or in a publishers' office instead of working as a freelance at home."

"Why didn't she?"

"Owen said she was needed at home. They couldn't find a satisfactory housekeeper after

Lorna died. As soon as Bridget left school, she took over the running of the house. It's a sad old business, that, Robert. The older I get, the clearer I see that one wrong step is like a stone thrown into a pool. The circles of trouble and unhappiness spread from it so widely, and the effects are irrevocable."

"What exactly did happen? I never knew, although Aunt Pamela once hinted dark things about Uncle Owen's thwarted love. Couldn't quite see him in the part of a lover. He's always seemed such a cold-blooded person. May I?" added Robert, taking out his pipe.

"If you must, dear. There's an ashtray on the window-sill. And perhaps you'd put some more coal on the fire before you sit down."

It was almost dark and the snow outside had taken on a blue tinge. Inside, the fire leapt and crackled as Robert added the coal, and long shadows danced across the ceiling.

"Your Uncle Owen wasn't always so cold and self-contained as he is now," went on Mirabel, "although he was always more reserved than any of the other children. And he had too much pride. Anyway, he fell deeply in love with Lorna Ashbury, who was introduced to him by Paul Armadale, his friend.

9

Owen courted Lorna with all the single-mindedness he has always brought to the things that matter to him, but she married Paul. It was a bitter blow to Owen, who refused ever to see Paul again. Paul was killed in the invasion of Europe in 1944, leaving Lorna with a two-year-old daughter, Bridget. They had been married only five years.

"Owen returned to the hunt. I think he wore her down. He seemed possessed of an iron determination. She married him three years after Paul's death. She had little money, a child to support, and she was tired of the struggle. I remember we had a talk just before they were married. I thought then, and she confirmed it herself later, that she ought not to have married Owen. She had loved Paul Armadale, and she didn't love Owen but married him for a home and security for her child. She did her best, but it was a wrong decision and it caused much unhappiness. Owen had been bitterly jealous of Paul while he lived, and when he succeeded in marrying Lorna, he found that in her heart she was still dedicated to her dead husband, so that Owen's jealousy lived on, and turned him against Bridget, too. If Lorna had borne him a child of his own, if might have helped. I don't know. However, she didn't. She adored Bridget and that added fuel to Owen's jealousy. Their home life was very strained, and Lorna's health, never very robust, gave way. Bridget was twelve years old when her mother died."

"A bleak outlook for the kid."

"Yes. I felt sorry for both Owen and Lorna, but of course I never interfered until I saw that Bridget was suffering for both of their sins. I promised Lorna to look after Bridget, and I tried to persuade Owen to let her come and live with us after Lorna died. I won't go into that. We quarrelled. It was very painful. Owen never forgave his wife for discussing their married life with me. His pride was affronted. He's kept his distance from me and the whole family since then. Although Bridget is loyal and never says anything against her home life, I believe Owen has made her pay for bearing the name of Armadale. That was why I was so glad when Felix came on the scene while she was still at school. And that's why I'm disturbed about this news of his engagement to Susan."

"Do you know him at all?"

"Only through Bridget's eyes. To her, he's a paragon. He came here once with her. A

11

tall, fair boy with a nice smile and kind eyes. I liked him. They seemed to be so easy together. I was glad for Bridget, and thought, here is someone who will make up for everything."

"The best thing for her now would be to get a decent job and discover that there are other young men in the world besides Felix Parvey, and other interests in life."

"Yes. I hope she won't be like her mother—always looking back. I shall try to stiffen her backbone if there's any weakness."

"The moral seems to be, keep your heart intact."

"That is difficult, but the head must be able to rule the heart, or life can be a sorry mess."

"And your head has never failed you, Grandma."

They were silent for a few minutes. Robert, leaning forward in his chair, nursing his pipe, was gazing into the fire. Mirabel, watching him, thought how like his father he was. The same dark, rugged looks, the same build, the same slow smile that always made her heart ache now when she saw it, so clearly did it bring her son back to her. And since the road accident which had killed his parents two years ago, Robert had lost the flippancy and a certain youthful argumentativeness that had sometimes irked her, and gained the quiet assurance which had been John's, so that the likeness between them was stronger than ever. In her grandson, she found her greatest consolation for the loss of his father. The past two years had placed heavy responsibilities on him and he had come out of them with great credit, but he now looked and seemed older than his thirty years.

Gwen broke the silence when she came in to fetch the tea-trolley and switch on the lamp.

"Cosy as it is here, I must be going soon," said Robert. "Can I see Grandfather for a few minutes?"

"Of course, dear. He'll be delighted to see you. Must you go this evening? Why not stay the night? It will be very unpleasant driving. It's still snowing."

"I know. And if I leave it till tomorrow, I may have to dig my way out of your drive. Don't worry. The main roads will be clear enough. I won't leave it much later, though. Just have a short natter with Grandfather."

While he was upstairs, the telephone rang and Mirabel answered it. She was always

13

concise and a little formal on the telephone, so that it was not a long conversation. She was hanging up the receiver when Robert came down.

"That was your Uncle Peter and Susan. She is marrying Felix on the last Saturday in March."

"Losing no time," said Robert. "Well, that's the first of your grandchildren to take the plunge, Grandma."

"Yes," said Mirabel, but she looked grave, and said no more about it.

Watching him envelop himself in his heavy tweed overcoat in the hall, she thanked him for coming.

"It's so good to see you, Robert. I can talk more freely to you than to any other member of the family, and it is such a help."

"It's my job—to be a good listener."

"And very well you perform it. I'm sure your practice will grow. You inspire confidence. That is a great asset. Oh dear, what a night! It's almost a blizzard. Telephone me when you get home, dear."

"Righto. Oakdene is only ten miles away, you know, and there is absolutely no need to worry."

Which was all very sensible, thought

Mirabel, as she watched the car move off down the drive, but she could never forget that his parents had driven off down the same drive little more than two years ago and had never reached their destination.

It was late that evening before she returned to her diary.

Peter telephoned. Belatedly, as I told him. Susan is marrying Felix Parvey at the end of March. Some children seem to be given all they want from the day they are born. Susan's has been a primrose path all the way; Bridget's a thorny one. And now this.

Robert came this afternoon. So happy to have him to myself for an hour. He is more like John than ever. I wonder why I can talk to my grandchild more freely than to my children. Why does the bond seem closer? It is not an uncommon experience, I believe.

A little tired. This birthday has had a chequered pattern.

2

WINTRY WEATHER

BRIDGET ARMADALE picked her way through the slush on the pavement of Ellarton High Street, keeping a wary eye open for the buses which sent showers of muddy spray in her direction as they roared up the hill. When she turned off into a narrow road, the slush was even worse, for it had never been swept and the snow had accumulated. She had only a short distance to go, however, before diving into the building which housed the offices of The Monitor. She waved a cheery greeting to two men and a typist as she passed through the outer office and went into the editor's room.

"Hullo, Felix. Sorry I'm late. My usual bus didn't run. I had to wait twenty minutes for the next. At least, I walked part of the way."

"Nice morning for a walk, I must say. What have you got for me?"

"The Out-and-About column and the article on Rushleigh church. It has an in-

16

teresting history. Afraid it's longer than you suggested. Hope we're not short of space."

She handed him the typescripts and sat on a corner of his desk while he answered the telephone.

"Any new ideas for me this week, Felix?" she asked when he had finished.

"No, Biddy. Not so far, anyway."

"Can I help Jim with the sub-editing?"

"Better ask him."

"You look a bit worried. Anything wrong, or just Monday-ish?"

"I'll tell you at lunchtime. I feel in an extravagant mood. We'll go to The Duke's Head."

"If I'd known, I'd have worn my Sunday best."

"You'll do."

Over lunch, Felix talked business, discussed the council meeting she had reported and made some encouraging comments about her column, but she felt all the time that his thoughts were elsewhere. She knew him too well not to notice it, but even then was miles from suspecting the truth.

"Let me guess. A publisher has made you an offer for your book, and that's what we're

17

celebrating," she said, as the waiter arrived with their coffee.

"Hardly, when it's not even finished."

"Well, I've seen so little of you out of office hours lately that I thought you might have finished it and sent it off, just to surprise me."

"No. In fact, I haven't touched it for weeks."

She looked surprised, and then, for the first time that morning, felt a chilly premonition of trouble.

"What is it, Felix? We don't have secrets."

"I've been trying to tell you for weeks," he said. He paused, then went on quickly, "We've always been such good friends, Biddy. Almost grown up together, you might say. But we've come to the end of a chapter. I'm engaged to be married to Susan."

"Engaged? To Susan? Susan who?" she asked stupidly.

"Susan Rainwood, your cousin."

"But . . . but you hardly know her."

"I told you. I bumped into your uncle and aunt and Susan when I was on holiday in October. They were staying in St. Mawes."

"But you were touring."

"I didn't go any farther than St. Mawes.

We saw a good deal of each other that week. And since."

"When I thought you were immersed in your book."

He rushed into speech again, driven by her white cheeks and incredulous eyes into a flow of platitudes.

"I knew you'd be surprised. We've kept it pretty dark, I know. But . . . well, we all grow up, Biddy. We've had good times together, you and I. It's meant quite a lot to us." His words died away under her anguished scrutiny.

"Quite a lot," she echoed. "Tell me one thing, Felix. When you said to me last September that we made such good partners that you hoped I'd let you make the partnership permanent and official when you became editor, what did you mean?"

"I was coming to that," he said eagerly. "Although you're a freelance, you do a lot in the office, sub-editing. I feel that you should be paid a proper salary for that and have your position regularised, so to speak, as a sub-editor."

"And you gave me a brooch to seal the pact the day before you went on holiday," she said gently, knowing that he had lied.

"Well, what about it?" he asked.

"No, Felix. You suggested that I should help Jim now and again with sub-editing because you thought it would help me as a journalist, and it has. But I can't give any more time than I have done in the past, and you know that doesn't warrant a paid post. You didn't have to think that up. But I'm grateful for all the help you've given me with my work."

Under her eyes, he dropped the pretences and said with an unhappy and apologetic air:

"It just bowled me over, Biddy. The very first day we spent together. I never knew it could be like that. You and I . . . You know how fond I am of you . . . but this is quite different."

She stopped him then. The whole thing had become a hideous embarrassment to both of them and she saw that to act it out was the only way. When he lied, she thought, perhaps he had only been trying to be kind, to spare her embarrassment as well as himself.

"Well, it's high time I congratulated you," she said, and forced a smile. "It's been such a surprise that I've really only just managed to take it in. I wish you both all the happiness in the world, Felix. You know that."

"Thank you, my dear."

"Have you announced it? I haven't heard a word from the family."

"We announced it this weekend. We plan to be married at the end of March."

"So soon? Well, Susan's a very lucky girl. Now I must be going. I won't come back to the office this afternoon. I've an article to finish for The Gazette."

"That'll be the fifth or sixth they've taken from you, won't it?"

"Yes. I seem to have found a little niche there."

"Well, keep up the good work. Will you be in again before next Monday?"

"Not unless you have any special assignment."

He walked to the bus-stop with her. They were both ill at ease.

"Don't wait, Felix. The bus isn't due for another ten minutes."

"All right. Be seeing you."

"Goodbye. Thank you for the lunch."

As her eyes met his, it seemed to her that she was looking at a stranger. This tall, fair man with the grey eyes and regular features no longer seemed to be the boy she had known so closely ever since she was a school-girl of thirteen.

"Goodbye, Biddy."

She watched him stride off down the street and disappear round the corner. A feeling of unreality gripped her. As she jogged home in the bus, she thought, thank goodness he at least managed to tell me before Father knew. I can be prepared, now. But quite how she was going to prepare herself, she did not know.

Dinner that evening was the usual formal, rather silent meal. Bridget, casting several uncertain glances at her stepfather, found it difficult to summon up the resolution to tell him the news, but she had decided that it must be done before he heard it from the family. Better wait until she had served coffee. He hated disturbed meals, for he treated food with respect, and demanded high standards of cooking, punctilious service and an elegant table. He sat opposite her now, fingering his glass of wine, immaculately dressed in the black pin-striped suit and white shirt that was his daily uniform. Tall, thin, handsome in a bloodless style, she had tried to love him, to establish some kind of affection between them, but had ended up baffled and shrinking from his sardonic, polite tongue. He had a brilliant brain, held an important position in the Treasury, and his work was his life. But of the man behind the civil servant, she knew nothing. He allowed her to know nothing.

When she brought in the coffee, he seemed to notice her for the first time.

"And did you pay your accustomed visit to Ellarton today?" he asked.

"Yes." With a steely effort, she managed to pass his cup without spilling any of the coffee. "I heard some news that may surprise you."

"Indeed? What might that be?"

"Felix is engaged to your niece, Susan."

He put down the cup that had been halfway to his lips.

"Felix Parvey to marry Susan? Well, that *is* unexpected news. Had you any inkling?"

"No. I haven't seen much of Felix lately, outside of business hours."

"You are admirably calm, my dear. Am I wrong in thinking that you had expectations in that quarter yourself?"

She was familiar with the gleam in his pale blue eyes. It was always there when he was placing his barbs.

"We're good friends, and always have been. No more than that."

"Really? Well, I must say that I'd got into the way of assuming that one day you and he would marry, if he ever earned enough to support a wife. At one time, he seemed almost to be living in the house."

"The wedding is to be at the end of March."

"Will you go?" he asked mockingly.

"If I'm invited," said Bridget, her head high as she met his look.

"Little doubt about that. My brother, I am sure, will want a large wedding in keeping with what he considers his status. We'd better sound the happy couple out about a wedding present. Shall I leave that to you? No, in the circumstances perhaps you would prefer me to consult Susan."

"Yes, I think that would be best."

"So we shan't be seeing Felix Parvey about the place in future. Well, Susan's a very attractive girl, and I dare say her father will cushion the nest for the young couple. He has more money than he knows what to do with. I wish you wouldn't start clearing the dishes while I'm still drinking my coffee, Bridget."

"I'm sorry. I thought you'd finished."

"I haven't. And I should like another cup. You make excellent coffee, my dear."

"I'm glad you like it. I tried a new kind."

"So I'd noted. It's very good. You don't seem to have enjoyed your dinner this evening. A pity. The sole was too good to be picked at."

"I had a large lunch. Felix took me to The Duke's Head to celebrate," she said, her eyes defiant now as anger at his sadistic pleasure in her news drove out the unhappiness that had threatened to swamp her.

"Did he? Rather inadequate consolation, surely. But never mind, my dear. It's all experience. Painfully, we learn."

"We learn what?"

"Why, not to expect much from people. The younger you are when you learn that lesson, the less painful your life will be. I congratulate you on producing such a delicious dinner in spite of the unsettling nature of your news. You've become a good cook, Bridget. A pity you don't manage the domestic help quite so efficiently. Did you tell Mrs. Hoffman about the cobwebs in my bedroom?"

"No. I removed them myself."

"There you are. How can you hope to get

25

better standards if you won't educate the woman?"

"The woman of fifty doesn't take kindly to being educated by someone young enough to be her daughter. I don't want to lose her. She isn't bad, and we might not get a replacement."

"A weak argument. People don't respect you for being soft, Bridget. However, you reap the consequences. By the way, I'd better increase your allowance next month. You'll want something special to wear at the wedding."

"There's no need, Father. Now that I'm earning more with my work, I don't need a personal allowance."

"Nonsense. You run this house for me and earn a salary, so you needn't behave as though I'm offering you charity."

But that's how you make me feel, she thought, twisting her hands together under the table-cloth as she said quietly:

"I'm sorry. I didn't mean to. You've always been very generous with money."

"Why not? You are my stepdaughter and my responsibility. There is no need for you to go short of anything you want. I shall double your allowance for next month. We haven't had a wedding in the family for a long time. In fact, the last one was Aunt Lucy's fifteen years ago, when you were eight."

"And Mother wore a ravishing delphinium blue silk suit. I remember it so clearly."

"Yes. She stood out. She was a very beautiful woman," he said coldly, and went out of the room.

Bridget leaned her head on her hands, suddenly exhausted by the battle. Sometimes it seemed as though all her encounters with her stepfather were battles under the surface. He had been pleased at her news. Pleased to know that she was hurt.

In her room that evening, she sat down on the bed with a feeling of despair in her heart. The photograph of her mother smiled down at her from the chest of drawers. He had made her unhappy, too. As a child, she had been all too conscious of the strain under their polite exchanges, had winced at the barbed remarks he so often aimed at her mother. But the climate of love which her mother had wrapped round her had kept his east wind at bay. Now his barbs were aimed at her, and without Felix to sustain her, she did not know how she could bear it.

She crossed the room and picked up the

photograph of her mother. He was right. She was beautiful, but unhappiness and poor health had already begun to show when that photograph was taken, and the eyes did not reflect the smile on the lips. If she had inherited her mother's looks, would Felix have? . . . She stifled the foolish thought. She had inherited nothing of her mother's looks, she thought, looking at her wan face in the mirror. On an impulse, she burrowed into the top corner drawer and drew out a faded photograph in a leather folder. In the service dress of a lieutenant in the Royal Artillery, her father looked very young. He had been twenty-eight when he was killed. Only five years older than she was now. Her mother had told her that she was uncannily like her father, and studying the photograph now, Bridget could see some likeness herself: the same short nose, full lips, dark eyes. His hair had been auburn where hers was a reddish gold. There the similarities ceased, as far as she could see. She did not remember him at all. She only knew that her mother had thought him a fine person. It was a kind face, and a strong one with that square jaw and wide forehead. And he had been robbed of so many years.

She put the photograph back and closed the drawer. Outside, the south-west wind which had brought the thaw buffeted the house and boomed through the trees. Had anyone, she thought, ever felt as lonely as she did in that house that night?

3

AN ALLY

WITH the wind in her face and the rain pouring down, Bridget cycled home from the library on the following Saturday afternoon, loaded with books on the history of Ellarton and its neighbouring villages. In the hall, she met her stepfather, who eyed her dripping figure with a frown.

"Did you have to cycle in this weather? I thought you said you were catching a bus to the library."

"I meant to, but I missed it. I couldn't wait an hour, and it wasn't raining much when I left."

He said no more. When she took tea into the sitting-room a little later, he was looking at one of her library books.

"By the way," he said, "Grandma Rainwood telephoned while you were out. Wanted to know if you would go to tea tomorrow. I said you'd telephone her and I had no idea whether you were free."

"Yes, I am."

"Well, you don't have to go. White lies are permissible. I don't suppose you are particularly anxious to talk about Susan's engagement and subject yourself to Grandma's probing."

He was right. The mere mention of Felix and Susan now was like hammering on a nerve, and a week of bad nights and desolate misery had left her feeling that all she wanted was a little hole to crawl into. But, sooner or later, she had to face it.

"I'll go. Grandma isn't easily put off."

"Well, if you take my advice, you'll keep your own counsel. The Rainwood family is a large one, and the grapevine works very well. There's nothing they like better than to chew over the private affairs of their relatives, and Grandma has always been convinced of her own wisdom in managing family matters. Unless you want to provide the cud for the family chewing, you'll give nothing away to Grandma. I speak from experience."

"You haven't ever given them anything to talk about, surely. You hardly ever see any of them."

"Enough. And Grandma seizes the smallest opportunity to lecture and instruct."

"I know she's rather an autocrat, but I've always found her kind and just."

"Who wants to feel like a defendant in a magistrate's court? However, it's up to you. And if the weather's bad, for heaven's sake don't cycle tomorrow and turn up at Bredon Lodge looking like the poor little orphan Grandma likes to think you are."

"Not from anything I've ever said."

He gave her an odd glance, then said:

"Well, I've warned you. These books look interesting. Are you doing an article based on them?"

"Yes. A series of six on the history of the neighbourhood for The Monitor."

"I must read them when they come out. No, I won't have another cup of tea, thank you. I shall be working in the study, and shan't want anything more today."

"Shall I bring you some coffee later?"

"Thank you."

When he had gone, she poured herself another cup of tea and leaned back in her armchair. What a strange, difficult man he was! For a moment or two just now, she had felt that they were allies. She knew that when he read her work, he would bring all his keen, analytical intelligence to bear on it. His criticisms were always pertinent, his praise rare but highly prized for that reason. And the odd thing was that just then, she preferred his detached stringency to the kind probing which she feared she would meet from Grandma Rainwood.

The presence of Grandfather Rainwood at tea the next day helped, for, because he was ill at ease with the younger generation, he was always particularly polite to them, and the formal atmosphere he generated kept at bay all but superficial matters for discussion. It was his first afternoon downstairs after his attack of lumbago, however, and he retired early.

Now for it, thought Bridget, as Grandma Rainwood returned to the drawing-room after seeing that he had all he wanted.

"You're not looking well, Bridget. Susan's engagement to Felix has been a bad blow to you, I'm afraid. Had you no idea?"

"None."

"I see. Felix must have been at some pains to conceal it from you, then."

"Would you mind if we didn't talk about it,

Grandma?" asked Bridget desperately. "It's very painful, and I'd rather not."

"I dare say," said Mirabel with the calm assurance of a nurse dealing with a protesting patient, "but it often helps to release your feelings, however painful, and I want to help. To do that, I must know one or two facts."

"The facts are that I misunderstood the position. Foolish of me. You haven't told anybody else, I hope."

"Only Robert. He was here last week, and when he told me about Susan and Felix, I couldn't conceal my surprise and dismay."

"I wish you hadn't."

"I told him that it was to go no further, and you can rely absolutely on his discretion."

"Perhaps. I shall be surprised if there's no gossip among the family, though. Father warned me."

"It will not be through Robert or me," said Mirabel firmly. "And your father mistakes concern for inquisitiveness. However, if it is only your pride that is hurt, there is no need to feel anxious about you."

"I'm sorry, Grandma. I'm just feeling like a piece of chewed string."

"He meant a great deal to you, didn't he?"

"Yes. It grew over ten years. They're not easily wiped out."

"It's a pity, dear, that you've led such a secluded life. I blame myself for not drawing you closer into the family. You have so many cousins of all ages to make up for the lack of brothers and sisters. Your father has kept aloof, I know, and that's his business. But if you'd had more friends, a different home life, you wouldn't now be left so shipwrecked. However, ifs are no help. We must be practical. You need a change of work. New interests."

"I like my work."

"You won't go on working for The Monitor now, will you?"

"I hadn't thought of anything else."

"Is that wise? To go on working for Felix?"

"Why not? We are still friends and colleagues in work."

"That is not the way to forget him."

"But I don't want to forget him."

"That is very foolish. It's merely rubbing on a wound. Asking for trouble."

"I'm sorry, Grandma, but feelings can't be so conveniently organised."

"They can be guided by a little rational thought. However unhappy you are about it,

35

the only sensible thing to do is to put Felix out of your life. You're young, with your life before you. It's futile to keep grieving for the past. Your mother did that, and much unhappiness it brought. I expect you to have more grit, Bridget."

Bridget lifted her hands in a little gesture of helplessness, aware that her head was aching and that shivers were running up and down her spine. Just then, far from having any grit, she felt like a limp piece of seaweed in the strong current of Grandma Rainwood's personality. How good-looking the old lady was, she thought, with her classical features, white hair and tall, slim figure. The severity of the face was redeemed by the dark blue eyes which expressed a warm interest in life. Bridget had known that face on rare occasions to reflect a compassion so deep that it seemed to embrace all the pain of the world, although usually it conveyed an impression of judicial calm. Her stepfather's reference to a magistrate was apt enough.

"Well, I have a suggestion to make," went on Mirabel, as Bridget said nothing. "Robert knows the director of a group of women's magazines. They happened to be lunching together last week and he mentioned the difficulty of getting good editorial staff. They're looking for someone now and Robert is willing to give you a letter of introduction."

"And what will Father say at the prospect of coming home to a cold house and no dinner?"

"I've thought of that. Gwen thinks her sister might be willing to take on the job of cook-housekeeper. She lives quite near you, and since her husband died a year ago, things haven't been easy for her."

"It's very kind of you to bother, Grandma, but it wouldn't work, you know. Father is a perfectionist. He would never keep any domestic staff if I wasn't there to make good any deficiencies. And we're really all quite satisfied as we are. Being a freelance fits in very well with my home responsibilities, and I prefer the variety and freedom of my work to an office job."

"Well, why not think it over?"

"No, Grandma. Thank you all the same."

Mirabel had not expected her to be so firm, and her voice had a little edge to it as she said:

"I think you're unwise to keep your connection with The Monitor, anyway, Bridget. You will be well advised to put Felix out of your life. I wouldn't say this if I didn't believe that your feelings for him run very deep. And I don't underestimate the difficulty. But at least do what you can to help yourself. I know you think I'm old and have forgotten what it's like to be in love. But experience teaches you the utter futility of not cutting your losses. And I do know how painful that is. But it must be done. Now we'll say no more about it. Robert is coming over this evening to discuss a business matter with Grandfather and I must look out some papers for him, so if you'll excuse me for a few minutes, dear."

Bridget's reception of Robert when he arrived a little later was wary. Pride it might be, but she writhed at the thought of having been the object of their discussion that week. She had seen little of him since her childhood days, when her mother had kept in contact with all the Rainwood relatives. At the few family functions she had attended since her mother's death, her encounters with Robert had been brief. Whatever he had heard about her that week, however, his manner was easy and pleasant, and he received the news that she was not interested in an introduction to the magazine group with a polite:

"I understand. The connection is there, if you ever need it."

He spent some time upstairs with her grandfather. When he rejoined them in the drawing-room, he said:

"Grandfather is a little tetchy. I gather Great-Uncle Arthur paid him a visit this morning."

"Yes. I tried to put him off, but he insisted on seeing Charles, and thoroughly annoyed the poor dear by pointing out that if he were not so addicted to fresh air and exercise, he wouldn't have lumbago."

"What should we do without Great-Uncle Arthur to stir up the pot?"

And at that moment, there was a loud knocking on the front door. Mirabel went to open it, and Bridget's face went as white as chalk when she heard the voices in the hall. To meet Felix and Susan now, she thought, was beyond her. She stood up, her head swimming, and looked round almost desperately. Then she felt Robert's hand on her shoulder.

"Come on. Hoist the flag. Rainwoods don't run away."

"I'm not a Rainwood."

"Then let's see what the Armadales are made of."

He had hold of both her shoulders now and she looked up at him appealingly, all defences down in this emergency.

"Help me," she whispered.

"I'll do my best. Chin up."

When Susan and Felix came in, Bridget was back in her chair, pale, but smiling. She had not seen Felix since he had broken the news to her. He looked uncomfortable when he saw her, but Susan looked radiant and Bridget wondered whether she imagined the gleam of triumph in her dark brown eyes when they exchanged greetings.

"We just had to present ourselves to Grandma and say we're sorry for springing it on everybody," said Susan.

"So I should think," said Robert. "Not least, for springing it on your employer. All our training wasted. I shall have to put a ban on pretty typists. They get married too soon."

Susan smiled up at him teasingly.

"You won't be affected. I never got within yards of you. Your paragon, Miss Cornelian, will never forsake you, Robert."

"I hope not."

"She adores you, and you know it."

"I do not. My secretary is a very sensible, level-headed woman. No need to think everybody is moonstruck just because you are."

"Dear Robert. I shall miss the office. That's the only teeny-weeny regret I have."

"Well, my congratulations, Parvey, and best wishes to you both."

"Parvey! How formal can you be? Felix is one of the family now, Robert," said Susan.

Robert eyed Felix with calm detachment, as though weighing up this new-comer to the family, and said:

"You haven't left yourselves long to find a home."

"Daddy is buying a house that's just come on the market at Oakdene. You'll know it, Robert. The white house with the green shutters on the corner of Gander Lane. We went over it on Wednesday evening, and fell in love with it. Spent an hour there yesterday, to see it in daylight, and were quite sure about it. Daddy's giving it to us for a wedding present. Aren't we lucky?"

"Some wedding present," said Robert, smiling. "It's a handsome house. Quite a bit of ground, there, too, I believe."

"About an acre. Daddy's going to get in

touch with you tomorrow about the legal side."

"I'm glad you're staying within easy reach of the family, dear," said Mirabel.

"Daddy was adamant about that. The Rainwoods stick together, he said. And when you come to think of it, we do. We all live inside a circle of no more than fifteen miles diameter."

"With Grandma sitting at the centre of the web," said Robert. "Can you get early possession of the house, Susan?"

"As soon as the legal formalities can be put through. The owner is moving out at the end of this month. I can't wait to furnish it. Felix doesn't have much spare time, so he's leaving it all to me, and as you're kindly releasing me from the office after only a week's notice, I can start shopping straight away."

"I'm not aware that I had much choice. You'd wheedled your way round Mr. Trawler, and he's the one who'll be inconvenienced."

"Well, we must drink to your happiness," said Mirabel. "Robert, dear, would you play host? It's Gwen's evening out. You know where everything is. It's a pity your grandfather can't join us, but I don't think I'll disturb him any more today. He's had rather a tiring day."

"You'll be bringing your article into the office as usual tomorrow, Biddy, won't you?" asked Felix, while Robert busied himself with bottles and glasses.

"Yes, I was going to post it, but it's a bit longer than usual and you may want to cut it, so I'd better come along."

"Good. Jim Travers went off sick on Friday. I may need you if he's not back tomorrow. Could be 'flu."

"No shop tonight, darling," said Susan, sitting on the arm of his chair, and putting her arm round his shoulders.

Happiness had put an extra bloom on her, thought Bridget. The jade green dress she was wearing suited her creamy skin and jet black hair, and its narrow waist and full skirt flattered the dainty lines of a figure that was petite but perfectly proportioned.

Bridget forced herself to ask more about the house that was to be their home and Susan chattered happily away to her. Toasting their happiness, she was able to smile as she met Susan's eyes, and knew then that she had not been imagining things. The old order is changed from now on, that look said. Bridget, glancing away, was aware of Grandma Rainwood's grave scrutiny.

"Well, I'm very sorry to break up this happy gathering," said Robert, "but I brought some papers home from the office to read this weekend, and I haven't looked at them yet. I'll drop you home on my way, Bridget. It's no night for hanging about for buses."

"Thank you, Robert. That's kind of you."

In the hall, Bridget was surprised when Grandma Rainwood took her in her arms and held her closely for a moment, for she was not a demonstrative woman. From the open door of the drawing-room, Susan's laughter rang out.

"Goodbye, my dear," said Mirabel, and patted her shoulder as she released her.

"Well done," said Robert, holding her coat for her.

As they went out through the vestibule, Bridget half-stumbled over something soft. Picking it up, she saw that it was the blue woollen scarf she had knitted for Felix years ago. And suddenly the odd sense of unreality which had helped her through the last hour dissolved and she was hard up against the brutal reality. Blinded by tears, she hung the

44

scarf up on the peg and followed Robert out to the car, thankful for the rainy darkness of the night.

For the life of her, she could say nothing on that drive home. All the control which she had clamped down on herself the previous week to withstand her stepfather's ironic attitude now crumbled like a weak dam before the torrent of her grief. Felix had been wearing that scarf one evening the previous summer when he had taken her out in his draughty old car, and had transferred it to her when she was cold. She remembered how he had gravely wound it round her neck and held both ends to draw her to him for the first kiss he had ever given her. "You're a part of my life I couldn't do without, Biddy," he had said.

Mercifully, apart from a comment on the weather which called for no reply, Robert was silent, too, on that drive home. She murmured an almost incoherent "Thank you" and slid out of the car as soon as it stopped, but he got out, too, and caught her by the gate. She looked away, but he took her by the shoulders, gently but firmly, and in the light of the nearby street lamp, saw her ravaged face.

"Nothing is ever as bad as it seems to be," he said. "You're too young to look like that."

But she was beyond words, and shaking her head blindly, she slid away through the gate. Fumbling in her bag for the key, she saw him still standing there by the gate. She lifted a hand in a shaky little gesture of farewell, and went in, groping like a blind person.

4

WEDDING DAY

MIRABEL, securely anchored in an armchair in the least congested corner of the room, a glass half full of champagne in her hand, surveyed the noisy throng of wedding guests with a wry detachment. She did not much like these hotel buffet affairs and would have preferred her grand-daughter's wedding reception to have taken place in her own home with a proper luncheon which could be eaten at a table in comfort instead of these bits and pieces pecked on the wing. But times had changed, and births, deaths and wedding receptions seldom now took place in the home, where she would always feel they rightly belonged.

She looked at the bride, smiling and vivacious and completely self-possessed on the far side of the room. Susan, the first of her grandchildren to marry. How pretty she looked in that long, full-skirted dress with the high neck and long, tight sleeves. Not so very different in style from Mirabel's own wedding dress, and Susan's waist span was no smaller than her grandmother's had been on that occasion. And it was Mirabel's pearl tiara which held the bride's tulle veil in place. Her daughters had worn the tiara at their weddings, and now her grand-daughter wore it fifty-three years after its first appearance on a bride. She winced at this reminder of the passage of time. Where had it all gone?

She pulled her mind back to the present. Too easily these days her thoughts turned to the past. It was a bad habit. She had no intention of contracting out of the present. Susan was smiling up at the bridegroom now. Felix, tall, fair, a little pale, stooped over her with a protective air as he talked. There was no doubt they were deeply in love. She wondered to what extent he was to blame for misleading Bridget. Easy to mistake affection for love. At the thought of Bridget, her heart ached and she looked round the room for the girl who had been so much in her thoughts lately.

"Hello, m'dear. You're looking worried. Anything wrong?"

Mirabel looked up at the tall, stringy figure of her husband and smiled.

"No, dear. Rather glad to have found myself a quiet corner. Have you managed to get something to eat?"

"Much as I want. Don't care for these fancy odds and ends. Can't even find a decent, plain sandwich. What a crowd! Don't know where Peter and Joyce have found them all."

"Well, twenty-two of them are either Rainwoods or married to Rainwoods."

"Good heavens! Are we really so prolific?"

"You should know, Charles."

"Can't keep track of them all."

"Let me refresh your memory. You have five children, all married, and ten grandchildren. And you have a brother."

"Don't bring him in. I've been trying to steer clear of Arthur all day. Well, they all do you credit, my dear, I'm sure. Pity your brother and sister can't be here to complete the tribe. Heavens, I'm hot! No air in this place. Why can't they open some windows?"

"If you add the Rainwoods to the relatives of the bridegroom, though he doesn't seem to have many, and then add some friends, you can see why there's a crowd," said Mirabel, who liked to bring her expositions to a conclusion.

"Quite. Well, if I can't fetch you anything,

my dear, I shall take a turn in the garden out there. Need some fresh air."

"Do that, Charles. There's nothing I want. You haven't seen Bridget, have you?"

"Bridget? No, m'dear. Do you want her?"

"It doesn't matter. Don't be outside too long. They'll be cutting the cake soon."

She looked after him, a little smile hovering at her lips. Even at seventy-five, his back was straight, his head erect, his movements, if a little stiff, still suggesting a man who set great store by physical fitness. Dear Charles. He had altered so little over the years. An honourable, good, but unimaginative man, born towards the end of the Victorian age and still in mind and spirit far closer to the Victorians and Edwardians of his youth than to later generations.

"Where's Father off to?"

Mirabel turned to the portly, middle-aged man beside her. Peter had the wrong figure to look well in morning dress, she considered.

"He wanted some fresh air, dear."

"Enjoying yourself, Mother?"

"Very much. Your daughter makes a lovely bride."

"Yes. Like to have kept her with us a bit longer, but what can you expect, with a pretty girl like Susan? Went off very well, I thought. The ceremony."

"The marriage service is always a moving one."

"Joyce shed a tear or two, I expect. She was a bit tearful last night. Our girl means so much to us."

"She's not moving far away," said Mirabel a little dryly, for she considered that Peter and Joyce had pampered Susan to a foolish degree ever since she had been born.

"And she's chosen a nice young man. Not very pushing, and I'm not denying that I'd expected a rather more ambitious choice from young Sue, but there, it's her happiness that matters and there's no doubt about that. Felix is an intelligent chap. I'll be able to help him to a better career. He's wasted running that tin-pot little magazine."

"How very distinguished Owen looks," said Mirabel, who had the habit of changing the subject abruptly if she disapproved of what had been said, a habit which annoyed her children but left them helpless.

"Doesn't often honour the family with his presence. He wears well, I must say," said Peter grudgingly.

"Who wears well?" asked a cheerful voice

51

as a dark-haired, fresh-complexioned woman in a pink coat and a pink feathered hat joined them.

"Hullo, Pamela. I was referring to Owen."

"I can't see him. Where is he?"

"Over by the window behind the buffet, surveying the throng in his usual supercilious manner."

"M'm, yes. Swooningly immaculate. He's kept his figure, Peter, which is more than you have," said Pamela, regarding her brother with amused affection. "And you're going grey. But never mind, you have a more youthful spirit."

"Should hope so. Owen's about as lively as a dead fish. And if I lived cloistered in the civil service instead of having to work for my living in the rough old world, I'd not be grey before my time."

"Owen works very hard," said Mirabel.

"The wizard of economics, and hasn't a clue about how any business is run. Heaven preserve me from the experts!" said Peter.

"Now, now, on this happy wedding day, let's have no carping," said Pamela. "This rough old world hasn't treated you so badly, by the look of things."

Peter grinned and patted his sister on the shoulder.

"But I'm in trade. The only Rainwood not to go in for a profession. I'll never live that down with Mother and Dad, however successful my business."

"Console yourself with the champagne and the Jaguar," said Pamela.

"Susan is trying to attract your attention, Peter," said Mirabel.

"Right. Duty calls. Enjoy yourselves," said Peter expansively, and began to worm his way through the crowd towards his daughter.

Mirabel eyed her eldest daughter with approval.

"You're looking very nice, Pamela. That colour is most becoming."

"Not too kittenish at my age?"

"Certainly not. You're still a young woman."

"Forty-five doesn't have a young ring about it, Mother. My son gave me a very old-fashioned look when he saw my hat. I could read his thoughts."

"Rupert is at the priggish age."

"Bless you, Mother, what a pillar of support you are! Isn't old Peter just loving this? Hope to goodness he spares us a long speech when he proposes the toast, but I fear the worst. I said we ought to have had Uncle Arthur. That would have been just something. But Peter wouldn't miss the chance of making a speech for worlds."

When Pamela moved away to speak to a friend, Mirabel resumed her study of the crowd and saw Bridget at last. She was standing by a pillar close to the buffet, talking to a burly man in horn-rimmed spectacles whom Mirabel did not know. She looked paler than usual, but composed, and attractively dressed in a pale blue silk suit with a matching pillbox hat. In a few moments, the burly man was drawn off and Bridget was alone. A curious blank expression seemed to make a stranger of her, then Rupert and Alison joined her and immediately she was smiling and talking to these two cousins as though she hadn't a care in the world. Mirabel applauded her courage, but sensed the enormous effort the girl was making.

"My grandmother is looking very regal today," said Robert.

"Thank you, dear. What a lovely spring day this is! Perfect for a wedding."

"They make an attractive pair, don't they? I thought you were looking a little bothered when I came up. Anything wrong, or just the effect of this din? The human voice *en masse* is pretty shattering."

"No, nothing wrong. I was just keeping an eye on Bridget."

"Where is she?"

"Over by the pillar."

Robert's eyes found her and studied the straight, slender back presented to him. As he watched, Felix and Susan, circulating, came up to Bridget. They laughed and chatted to her for a few minutes. Bridget had half-turned at their approach and was smiling and talking with apparent ease, but she held one hand behind her back all the time, and Robert could see it clenching and unclenching round the white gloves she carried. It worked ceaselessly on the gloves as though in a paroxysm all the time she talked. Then Susan and Felix went on their way, and he saw the hand relax and hang limply at her side. Turning to look down at his grandmother, he realised that she, too, had observed the exchange.

"I can see your Great-Uncle Arthur heading for Bridget, and he has the touch of an elephant. Shall we rescue her?" asked Mirabel.

The three of them converged on Bridget at the same time. After chatting together for a few minutes, Mirabel said:

"Arthur, would you be kind enough to give me an arm out to the terrace? I want to see where Charles has got to, and I'd like a little air."

Arthur Rainwood's grey eyes gleamed suspiciously beneath their bushy white brows as he looked at his sister-in-law's calm face. It told him nothing.

"All right, Mirrie. But I'm not hanging about outside looking for Charles and catching a chill. Prefer smoked salmon and champagne in the warm myself. And I'm not missing the wedding cake . . ."

Protesting, he went off with Mirabel in the direction of the french doors to the terrace.

"I've been hoping to have a word with you, Bridget," said Robert. "As the journalist of the family, I wonder if you could spare me a few minutes to talk shop."

Looking up at him, her dark grey eyes seemed bewildered and he suspected that she was exercising such rigid control over herself that there was no flexibility left to grasp what was required of her. Then she recovered and said:

"What did you say, Robert? Sorry, I was day-dreaming."

"It looks a little less congested behind that trough of flowers," said Robert as his arm was jogged by a passer-by.

He steered her there with a purposeful air and stood in front of her like a guard dog. She seemed to relax as they talked.

"But I'm only a small-time journalist," she said. "A weekly article for The Monitor and a few bits in the local paper now and again don't add up to much."

"I wouldn't call it a bad start. You're young to get into print."

"If you're really interested, Felix is the person to ask. Or your friend in the magazine world."

"He's abroad just now, and he's on the management side. I'd like the humble beginner's angle. A client of mine has a daughter who wants to go in for journalism and he was asking my advice," said Robert quite truthfully, although consultation with Bridget had never entered his head until five minutes ago, when he had decided that she needed help to get through this punishing ordeal.

"I see. Well, I love the work but it's usually a long time before you can earn very much. I was lucky. Felix is a first-class journalist and he taught me a lot."

"Have you any ambitions beyond The Monitor?"

"No. It suits me. I'm not on the staff, you know. Only a freelance contributor. But since Felix has been editor, I've had more space."

Felix, thought Robert. She had to keep bringing Felix in.

"What sort of articles do you write? I'm afraid we don't take The Monitor."

"Oh, a regular Out-and-About column, which speaks for itself. And bits of local history. I'm doing some research now for a series on the local history of Ellarton and its surrounding villages within a radius of about ten miles."

"In other words, Rainwood country."

"Yes. Felix has suggested six articles, but I may need more."

"Hullo, they're cutting the cake, and you've no champagne for the toasts," said Robert.

He lifted a finger to a waiter and obtained a glass for her. They shared a plate for their two pieces of wedding cake. The room fell silent for the bride's father. Robert shifted his feet, aware of the closeness of the atmosphere

58

and the heavy scent of the hyacinths in the trough close by. Uncle Peter was long-winded and rather pompous. Felix, replying to the toast, made a good speech. Glancing down at his companion, Robert surprised an expression of pain on her face that shocked and in some vague way irritated him. She was watching Felix. In a different mood, he thought, she could be attractive. The combination of that fair skin and red-gold hair with such dark eyes was unusual, and she had a good figure, slender and a little above average height. But just then she was too pale, with dark shadows under her eyes, a droop to her mouth, and shoulders which denied all the vitality suggested by her colouring. In the past he remembered her as a skinny, elusive child with a red pigtail, who had once retaliated with unexpected fierceness when he had teased her, and it had taken all of his fourteen-year-old strength to hold off the attack of the seven-year-old slip of fury. Subsequent encounters had been milder but not especially cordial. When, after a gap of several years, he had seen her at his grandparents' golden wedding celebration, he thought she had blossomed out rather well from that rather plain bud. Now, she looked wilted. Then, as he looked, he saw her shoulders stiffen and her head lift, so that he noticed the slender line of her throat and the good slope of her shoulders. Susan and Felix stood before them.

"Just had to have a few words with my favourite man before I change," said Susan, smiling up at Robert. "I missed you when you came in."

"I was ferrying the last of the guests. A splendid wedding and a beautiful bride," said Robert.

Susan's cheeks dimpled and she slid her hand under Felix's arm as he said:

"She's been far more composed than I have. Hope you've managed to get something to eat in all this scrimmage, Bridget."

"I have, thank you," said Bridget, who hadn't eaten a crumb. "A lovely wedding."

"But you haven't eaten any cake," said Susan. "You must. It's lucky, you know."

"I will. Have you managed to sort out all the Rainwoods, Felix? Rather a large family to assimilate."

"Pretty well. My wife's worked hard on me these past weeks and I've been given a thorough introduction all round."

"He's soon cottoned on to the relationship, Susan," said Robert, smiling.

"Yes. I'm really beginning to believe it now."

"So I should think," said Felix, putting his arm round her shoulders. "Did you know that Susan is wearing the tiara that her grandmother wore at her wedding, Biddy?"

"No," said Bridget. "It's very handsome and suits you beautifully, Susan. This is quite a day for Grandma Rainwood. And doesn't she look impressive?"

"I'm no fashion expert," said Robert, "but I'd give Grandma's hat top marks in this assembly. It's the sort Queen Mary used to wear, judging from the photographs I've seen, and Grandma looks every bit as regal."

"A toque," said Bridget.

"A what?" asked Robert.

"A toque. That's what those hats were called," said Bridget, looking at the crown of Parma violets on Grandma Rainwood's head, now visible by the window.

"I have an idea those cousins of yours are hatching up some mischief for our send-off, darling. Better get moving. We ought to be away by four," said Felix.

Susan and Felix left them, and Robert saw

Bridget sway, spilling the champagne from her glass. He took her arm, steadying her, and she recovered immediately.

"Have you had anything to eat?" he demanded bluntly, taking the glass from her.

"I'm not hungry."

"Maybe not, but we can't have you passing out."

"It's nothing. Just the heat."

He shepherded her through the french doors, found her a wooden seat behind a tub of holly, and made her promise not to move. When he returned with a plate of canapes and a glass of tonic water, she was sitting just as he had left her, looking out across the hotel garden, her hands folded in her lap.

"Thank you, Robert. It's kind of you, but I'm . . ."

"Not hungry. I know. Eat them."

She obeyed like a child, too exhausted to protest, while he watched her with calm detachment. They returned to the reception just in time to see Felix and Susan leave. Somebody thrust a bag of confetti into Bridget's hand and she found herself one of the laughing crowd on the hotel steps as Susan, in a turquoise blue coat and hat, dived for the waiting car, followed by Felix, who turned for a moment, smiling, the sun burnishing his fair hair. Then he lifted his arms in futile protection as confetti showered over his grey suit, and disappeared into the car. Automatically, Bridget followed the car down the drive behind a group of the brightest and most energetic of the young guests. Walking slowly back to the hotel after the car had disappeared, she found Robert still beside her.

"Well, that's that," he said affably. "Wonder where they're going. Any idea?"

"No. Abroad, I think. Hullo, Father."

"Well, Bridget. Are you ready to go now? Horrible anti-climax after the bride and bridegroom have left. The sooner we disperse, the better. That is, unless you are joining the family party at Uncle Peter's house. I rather assumed that the celebrations had gone on long enough for you, as they have for me."

"Yes, I'm ready. I must just say goodbye to Uncle Peter and Aunt Joyce, and Grandma. I'll meet you at the car in five minutes."

"Don't be longer. The other cars can't get away until I move."

Bridget turned to Robert as her stepfather left them.

"Goodbye, Robert. And thank you for being so kind."

"There's only one right and sensible thing to do, you know. Forget him," said Robert quietly.

She turned wide, protesting eyes to him, and then had gone, slipping through the crowd, and he did not see her again.

"Hi, there! You've been very taken up with our half-cousin by marriage, if that's what she is. I've been trying to work out the relationship," said a cheerful voice, and Robert turned to see his young sister.

"Hullo, Kit. Enjoyed yourself?"

"So-so. I'm not really much of a hand at social functions. Grandma has just read me a little lecture on not having gloves. I told her I'd spilt a cup of coffee down my skirt and mopped it up with my gloves, but I don't think she was impressed. Ladies don't spill coffee, and if they do, they don't mop it up with gloves and hide the gloves in a pot with a palm. Just look at my skirt."

She stood before him, a thin girl with a lively face. The skirt of her pink linen suit had a pale brown stain like a map of Britain stretching from halfway down the front to the hem. Beneath the Breton straw hat a pair of

64

large hazel eyes regarded the damage with amused resignation. It was an odd, quirky face, heart-shaped, with a brown complexion, a short nose and a wide mouth. Beneath the hat her face was framed with thick brown hair hanging rather untidily almost to her shoulders.

"Pity to ruin a pair of gloves as well as the skirt," observed Robert.

"I know. Just used them on the spur of the moment, without thinking. It's no use. I shall never be an ornamental Rainwood. Grandma will have to resign herself to that. I have."

"It doesn't bother you a great deal, I fancy," said Robert, thinking that at nineteen Christine had just the same coltish, flyaway look as the schoolgirl of fourteen. Her first year at the university in the west country had added no gloss of sophistication to her frank, gauche manner.

"No. Just a passing fancy now and again that it would be pleasant to look as attractive as Susan and be as pleased with myself as she is. Didn't she look every bridegroom's dream? He was well up to standard, too. Is he as intelligent as he looks?"

"I wouldn't know."

"What have you been up to with Bridget?

Consoling her? I hear from the cousins that she was Felix's girl before our Susan annexed him. True?"

"Could be."

"I'm sorry for her. She looks as though she could be fun. What a life to be tied up to Uncle Owen! He gives me the shivers. He looks at you as though you're on a slide under his microscope and he doesn't much care for what he's seeing. He's not about, is he?" she added, lowering her voice.

"Luckily for you. That tongue of yours should be learning a little discretion by now."

"I know, but there's no need to sound like Grandma. Is Bridget coming to the party this evening?"

"No."

She shot a look at him. He was not often so uncommunicative with her.

"Pity. Even a family party would be better than an evening alone with Uncle Owen. If a man had given me the brush-off for another, I'm blessed if I'd mope about it. I'd go out and have a gay time and persuade myself that I'd had a narrow escape from the oblivion of domesticity."

"It's always blessedly simple to the on-looker. I suggest we discourage any gossip.

I'm gasping for a cup of tea. Let's see if we can find one."

"Good idea. I suppose we couldn't play hookey from this party and go up to the Festival Hall? There's a good concert on tonight."

"No. We're committed."

"What a pity you're so wedded to duty, Robert. We'd enjoy the concert so much more."

"I know," he said, taking her arm and steering her clear of a charging young Rainwood.

"And I've got to go back tomorrow, and I've seen hardly anything of you."

"You'll be home in ten days' time for the Easter vacation. We'll do some concerts then, if you've any time to spare from this field study group you're joining."

"I'll find time," said Christine, beaming at him.

Robert, sipping a cup of tea a few minutes later, felt suddenly out of tune with the occasion. Weddings went on far too long, he thought. Uncle Owen was right. He hoped he wouldn't hear any more gossip about Bridget and Felix Parvey that evening. He'd had enough of the subject.

5

OWEN RAINWOOD

BRIDGET, walking along the lane from the bus stop one evening towards the end of May, decided that this was her favourite month of the year. Wild parsley still fringed the lane with its white lace flowers and the first wild roses were blooming in the hedge. Everything was bright and fresh with the touch of spring still upon it while the lusher fulfilment of summer was beginning to add its deeper note. Across the quiet countryside came the distant call of a cuckoo. The sun, slanting across the meadow, caught the weathercock on the church steeple and burnished it to a rich copper colour. She felt happier just then than for weeks past, filled with love for this part of Surrey, which, knowing the by-ways and footpaths as she did, still offered countryside as beautiful and peaceful as it had been fifty years ago.

She was surprised to see a car outside the house, for visitors were rare.

Quickening her steps, she found Robert at the front door.

"Hullo," he said, as he saw her. "I was just about to give up here and go and look in the garden. Grandma asked me to bring this book over. She dug it up from Grandpa's library. Thought it might be useful."

Bridget thanked him and exclaimed with pleasure when she saw the book.

"I've been trying to track this down. Just what I need for the last in my series of articles. Won't you come in and have some coffee, Robert?"

"Thanks."

In the sitting-room, she studied the book more carefully.

"This is a find! I must show it to Felix. Look at this old map, Robert. Grandma's house is marked, and it was the only one in that part of Melbridge then."

She left him poring over the map while she made coffee. It was growing dark when she returned, and she switched on the lamp.

"Father's attending a conference in Belgium this week," she said. "He'll be back tomorrow."

"A bit lonely for you."

"Not really. I've been working at The

Monitor office all this week. The assistant editor has left, and Felix hasn't been able to get a replacement yet. I've been helping out."

"So I heard," said Robert a little dryly.

"Oh, did you?"

"Susan told me. I met her on the train yesterday. She'd been up to London for the day."

They were silent for a few moments. Bridget was conscious of Robert's thoughtful scrutiny, and found it disturbing.

"Are you thinking of taking the job on permanently?" he asked.

"Felix wants me to, and I'd like it, but Father has to be looked after. It would mean trying to do it on a part-time basis. If Felix can't get anybody, it may come to that. The Monitor can't afford to pay much, and it's hard to find the right person at our price."

"You identify yourself very closely with The Monitor, don't you?"

"I've known it from its beginning, when Stewart Lindsay and Felix started it up on a shoe string. Then Stewart pulled out, and Felix carried on. But it was Felix's baby, really. Stewart put up most of the capital, and Felix has built it up. Naturally I feel I'm part of it as I contributed to the first number."

"And when was that?"

"Four years ago."

"Parvey worked on the Ellarton News before then, I believe."

"Yes."

"I'd like to give you a word of advice, Bridget, and I hope you won't be offended."

"Go on."

"Don't take on a permanent job with The Monitor even if Felix can't get an assistant editor. It could lead to trouble."

"I don't understand."

Robert felt in his pocket for his pipe, seeking the right words. She had lost weight, he thought, and looked peaky. There was something about the dark grey eyes which were looking at him so gravely that made his task more difficult. At twenty-three, he thought, half irritated, she had no right to be so unsophisticated. He decided that there were no words to mask the blunt truth, and said firmly:

"Susan says you are still running after Felix, and I'm afraid that if you take on a regular job as his assistant, she'll cease to be amused."

Bridget's cheeks flushed scarlet at his words.

71

"But . . . but it's our work that makes the contact between us. Nothing more now. How can Susan be so unkind and unfair?"

"Be your age. Susan knows that you and Felix were very close friends."

"You must have had a nice gossip about me. Have you passed it all round the family?" she asked, suddenly angry with him for breaking the short spell of happiness which had been with her that evening.

"I'm only trying to help you avoid trouble in the future."

"I don't need your help," she flashed, "and I don't like your calm assumption that you know what is best for me."

"So you do still have a paddy," he said, smiling. "But the pig-tail's gone."

She turned away, trying to resist the unexpected appeal of that slow smile, and busied herself with drawing the curtains, saying:

"You always were a needling boy. I longed to get the better of you, and I never did."

"I had the advantage of years. Stop fidgeting with those curtains. You can't change uncomfortable facts by losing your temper. You don't have to reveal your feelings to me, but whatever your reason for keeping in touch

72

with Felix may have been, now that you know that Susan resents it, don't you think it would be foolish to invite trouble by taking permanent employment with Felix?"

"We're old friends. We share a working interest. What's wrong in that?"

"The only thing wrong is your lack of common sense. Put yourself in Susan's shoes."

"If I were married to Felix, and Susan was his friend and colleague at work, I should trust Felix absolutely. It would be insulting to him to do anything else."

"I believe you," said Robert, sighing. "You're too innocent for this world, Bridget. But, granted that Susan is jealous for no reason, the fact that she is jealous should be enough to stop you taking on this job. And I should have thought it better for your sake, too, to put Felix right out of your life. You're simply being unrealistic about this, you know."

"Would Felix have asked me to be his assistant editor if Susan would object? You must be making too much of her comments."

"Oh, Susan's playing it light, all right. Making a joke of it. But he must be obtuse if he hasn't any idea that she resents you, and I find it odd of him, to say the least, to make use of the girl he threw over, and more than a little unfair to her."

"It's your unpleasant mind that finds it odd. Being a solicitor perhaps makes you take a seedy view of people. Felix is an honest, kind person. He didn't throw me over, as you put it."

"Didn't you expect to marry him? I understood so."

"He was fond of me, as a friend. He made no secret of that, and never has. I assumed too much from that. Affection isn't the same as falling in love. When he met Susan, he realised the difference. That's all."

"And you?"

"He was my brother, my sister, my teacher, my friend. You don't understand. We've been friends for more than ten years. He was my only friend. I had nobody else, and wanted nobody else. You talk as though our friendship can be thrown away like a toy."

"Felix threw it away when he married. No wife's going to share that much of her husband with another woman, however platonic the friendship. Least of all young Susan, who has been spoiled all her life and is very possessive in her love. She won't spare you any crumbs of friendship from Felix to console you, and I think it's foolish of you to seek them. Where's the future in it?"

She looked down at her hands, suddenly weary. Calmly, inexorably, he had pinned her down like a butterfly on a board.

"You won't find a cure for love like that," he added gently.

"I expect you're right. I'll not take on that job. I assume Susan won't object if I post articles to The Monitor," she added bitterly.

"I'm sorry if I've upset you, Bridget, but I had to warn you before any harm was done. Susan was quite ready to smile about it when she told me, but underneath she was serious enough. Now let's forget it. I bought a copy of The Monitor last week and enjoyed your article on Rushleigh. I'm sorry I missed the earlier ones. Have you got any spare copies?"

"Yes, I can let you have them. The first two cover Ellarton. Oakdene, Melbridge and Lynwood are still to come. It took me longer than I expected, ferreting out all the material, but I've enjoyed it immensely. Suprising how much can be learnt from church records, and the vicar of Lynwood church was a wonderful source of information. He allowed me to borrow some old books and documents that opened up a very rich seam."

While they were talking about the history of the neighbourhood, they heard the front door close and a sound of footsteps in the hall. A minute or two later, Owen Rainwood came in.

"Hullo, Father," said Bridget. "You got back earlier than expected, then."

"Obviously," said Owen dryly. "Good evening, Robert. It's not often that you honour us with a call."

"I came with a book for Bridget from Grandma. You look tired, Uncle. A satisfactory trip?"

"Partially. Finished a little ahead of schedule, and just caught a flight back this evening."

"Can I get you something to eat, Father? What would you like?"

"Oh, I'll just have some coffee. I'm not hungry. No, don't go, Robert. Stay and have another cup of coffee with me. I'd like your opinion on a point of law."

"Right," said Robert, sitting down again.

"Coffee for two, please, Bridget," said her stepfather, glancing through the letters he had brought in from the hall and throwing them aside, unopened, as though they were of no interest.

Bridget presided over the coffee-pot in silence while the two men talked about some abstruse point in the law of contract. Afterwards, Robert tried to bring her into the conversation, shocked at the cold indifference his uncle had displayed to Bridget after a week's absence from home. She might have been a robot for all the interest he showed. But Bridget seemed to have taken on an armour of reserve since her stepfather's arrival and had little to say. She was very pale and this fact did seem to impinge on his uncle's consciousness at last, for as the clock struck ten, he addressed his first remark to her since his request for coffee.

"You look washed out, Bridget. Everything been all right while I was away?"

"Yes. Nothing to report."

"You ought to take Bridget with you on some of your trips, Uncle Owen," said Robert. "She could enjoy the sights while your nose is to the grindstone. A change of air and food might fatten her up. She looks as though a puff of wind would blow her away at present."

His uncle gave a thin smile as he said:

"I'm afraid there's nothing I can do. She's pining after a lost love, you know, like Aenone for her Paris."

"Father!" protested Bridget.

"Treading on corns? You mustn't be so sensitive, my dear. After all, I'm paying you the compliment of constancy. You inherit that admirable quality from your mother."

There was something in his voice and expression that made Robert's blood boil. His uncle seemed to be enjoying his step-daughter's discomfiture. His precise voice went on:

"Nothing to say? Well, we'll spare your blushes. I've a private matter I want to discuss with Robert, so, if you'll excuse us, Bridget, I'll take him off to my study."

"There's no need. I'm rather tired. If you don't mind, I'll go to bed."

"I don't mind, and I don't suppose Robert does."

Bridget picked up the tray and said goodnight. Robert opened the door for her. Resting a hand on her shoulder, he said:

"You won't forget to let me have those articles I missed, will you?"

"I won't. Goodnight."

Robert eyed his uncle with a calm distaste,

surprised that he should have anything of a private nature to discuss with him. As though aware of his thoughts, Owen said:

"It's a good many years since any member of the family has set foot in my house. Your father used to pay me an occasional visit."

"It's been your own wish to remain apart."

"Yes. Families are tiresome. The Rainwood family particularly so. However, I'll not enlarge on that. Your father was the best of the bunch. You're like him. To come to the point. I've decided it's time I made another will. Your father drew up the existing one, made before my wife's death. I had it in mind to go to another solicitor, not being in favour of these cosy family connections, but I haven't had time to look around, and as you've turned up tonight, you can save me the trouble. I imagine you're as discreet as your father, and as reliable."

"I should have thought it went without saying that you would receive the same treatment as the rest of our clients," said Robert coolly.

"Quite," said Owen, a little smile acknowledging this sally. "I would like you to be my executor. Would you be willing?"

"Certainly."

"Thank you. I've made precise notes on how I want my estate disposed of. I'll give them to you before you go tonight. Then if you'll let me know when you've drawn up the will, I'll come across to your office and sign it. I'd like you to keep it in safe custody."

"Right. Nothing you want to discuss?"

"No. It's all quite clear. You've had your hands full since your father died, I imagine."

"Yes. Mr. Trawler stayed on to see me through the worst. He's retiring in September."

"A bad thing, the way your father died. Such a waste. At fifty, he was in his prime. The Rainwoods are a long-lived family, too. He'd probably another twenty or thirty years in front of him. Not that one would wish to go on beyond one's useful time. When I can't work, I'd like to make my exit."

"The State won't be sparing you for some years yet," said Robert.

"Fortunately the brain doesn't deteriorate as soon as the body."

His uncle looked fit enough, thought Robert. Lived an austere life. A bit thin and drawn about the eyes, but quick in his movements, and not an ounce of superfluous flesh on him. Unwillingly, he had to concede a certain power in the personality of his intellectual uncle. There was penetration in his scrutiny, an incisiveness of manner that was impressive. Not endearing qualities, but Robert's legal mind could respect them.

"I like a whisky and soda for my nightcap. My sole alcoholic indulgence. Will you join me?" asked Owen.

"Thanks."

While his uncle was out of the room, Robert walked across to the portrait of his aunt, hanging in the centre of the wall. Even as a small boy, he had been impressed with the beauty of Aunt Lorna. A haunted kind of beauty, with her white skin, cloudy dark hair and mournful eyes. Always, the atmosphere in this house had been uneasy. There had been undercurrents which even the children had felt. Only when Aunt Lorna and Bridget visited the family on their own did the restraint drop, although there was always a gentle dreaminess about Aunt Lorna which seemed to keep her in a world apart. Bridget had treated her as though she was a piece of frail china, he remembered. Little things came back to him as he looked at the portrait. Things noticed almost unconsciously at the time, when he was a schoolboy, and never remembered again until now. His uncle had been regarded with awe and some fear by many of the young fry, for he carried with him in those days an air of barely controlled impatience, masked now in a cold urbanity. How little one knew of people, thought Robert. What really went on inside his uncle's clever mind and apparently cold heart?

"Here are the notes, Robert. No need to look at them now. How do you like your whisky?"

"Filled up with soda, please," said Robert, putting the envelope in his pocket. "This is a good portrait. Beautiful brushwork."

"A beautiful subject. Yes, it does justice to her, I think."

"She has a pre-Raphaelite style of beauty."

"Yes. You seem to be escaping the snares of matrimony, Robert," said Owen abruptly.

"Too busy to think of it."

"If you're wise, you'll stay too busy. Young Susan snapped up Felix Parvey as neatly as her father snaps up business sites. I doubt whether Felix will prove such a profitable investment, though."

"I don't know much about him."

"Oh, a nice enough chap, I suppose, but

82

spineless. He was the sun in Bridget's sky. She'll probably spend the rest of her life looking back at it."

"She's young. She'll get over it. Fall in love with two or three more before she's through, I expect."

"You underestimate the tenacity of the Armadale nature, and its peculiar liking for living with ghosts. No, my bet is that Bridget will make a little shrine for Felix and worship at it with a melancholy enjoyment all her life."

"It would do her good to get right away for a time, take a new job, meet fresh people. This is a pretty lonely life for her."

"And deprive her of her little visits to The Monitor? She wouldn't like that. And I couldn't spare her, you know. She's an excellent housekeeper and cook."

"You can hire a housekeeper," said Robert.

"But not one as good as Bridget. She's well paid, I assure you. No, it works very well, Robert, in spite of your grandmother's opinion that it's hard on Bridget. She has a comfortable home, and the time to do her writing, and she's not bad at it. In return, she sees that I'm not bothered with household affairs and provides me with an excellent dinner each evening. I don't think I ask too much in return for bringing up another man's child. She has all the money she needs and complete freedom. I don't interfere in her affairs at all."

The cold, analytical voice might have been presenting a balance sheet. Robert was aware that it left little comment open to him.

"It doesn't seem the best kind of life to help a girl get over a broken love affair. Solitude is the last thing that's wanted."

"But I've told you. She doesn't want to get over it. No, Robert. Our life here suits us both very well, whatever the rest of the family thinks. I need Bridget. She's my link with the past."

"A past you want to remember?" asked Robert bluntly.

"Certainly. We learn from the past. When we've reached the stage of being quite objective about it, of course. The last thing I would want to do is to forget the past, even if I could. Happily, I have reached the age when I can derive a good deal of wry amusement from it."

Driving home, Robert found himself in an unusual state of anger and dismay. No wonder Bridget had clung to Felix as to a lifeline, living in that atmosphere of cold inhumanity, the victim of a past for which she had no responsibility, the object of the unimpassioned revenge of an embittered man for the pain inflicted on him by her parents. All Robert's sense of justice was outraged, and when he remembered that he had been forced to destroy what was left of Bridget's connection with Felix, he decided that he must put something in its place, that she could not be left alone, with nothing to warm her life in that cold prison. When Christine came home for the summer vacation, he would rope her in. She was a warm-hearted, lively girl, who could have a tonic effect. Meanwhile, he would do what he could, and suggest to his grandmother that the need for help was greater than even she had appreciated.

6

CONVERSATION IN A GARDEN

IT was not until late the next day that
Bridget found an opportunity to tell Felix
of her decision. People had been in and
out of his office all day, and she had been
busy with galleys in the morning and layout
all the afternoon. She was sorry to have
to turn her back on work which she found
stimulating and an endless challenge to in-
genuity, but further reflection on Robert's
disclosure had convinced her that it was the
only thing to do. She hesitated about being
fully frank about her reasons, though, fearing
to cause trouble or embarrassment.

"I can't give the time the job will need,
Felix. You must count me out, although I'd
have enjoyed it if circumstances had been
different."

"We could adjust the hours for you, Biddy.
I thought you were half won over yesterday."

"I know. But not after thinking it over."

"That's a blow. You'll put in as much time

as you can spare until I can get someone, won't you?"

She hesitated, then said quickly:

"Not indefinitely. What about trying an agency?"

"Can't afford to pay much, that's the trouble."

"The Monitor's sales aren't dropping, are they?"

"No. Going up a bit. But . . . Well, the truth is, Biddy, I can't work for a pittance myself now that I'm married. Having a wife is an expensive business, I find. Sue's father wants me to give it up, you know, and take a job in his company."

"Oh no, Felix. You'd hate that. The Monitor means so much to you."

"Oh, I'm not going to agree, but it does make my case stronger if I can pay my way. Sue's been used to spending freely all her life. I can't expect her to pinch and scrape. So you see, if I can't get an assistant at my price, I shall have to do without. Any help you can give would be appreciated. Not that I want to use you for cheap labour, Biddy," he concluded with an apologetic smile, "but I know you enjoy the work, and it's good experience."

"You know I'd gladly work for nothing, Felix. I have an allowance from Father, and I earn a bit with odd articles. I shan't take any payment for work I do for you in the future, now that I know what your position is, but I don't think I ought to be your assistant, unpaid or not."

"Ought?" She was standing by his desk, her face troubled, and he took her hand. "You're hiding something. Come on, Biddy. You never could hide anything from me for long. Spill it."

"It's so cheap and petty. But . . ."

"Go on."

"Susan is going round saying that I'm still running after you, and I think she would resent it if I became a regular employee here."

"Who told you that?"

"Robert Rainwood. He met her on the train one evening."

"Oh, rot! Sue was joking. She's never shown any sign of being jealous. We're both as happy as crickets, and I'd know if anything was wrong."

"Maybe. But I don't like to have that impression spread about me. You know how these things get round the Rainwood clan."

"Oh, Robert's puffing up something quite trivial. What business is it of his, anyway?"

"He was just advising me to steer clear of you, for fear of causing trouble. I'd hate to do that for you, Felix. Perhaps it is a bit unrealistic to think that we can be friends, as before."

"My dear Biddy, this is a question of a job of work, no more. Why turn it down because of petty gossip? If anybody knows how Sue feels, surely I do. There's nothing in Robert's suggestion. Sue's a bit tactless with her sense of humour sometimes, but she never intended it to be taken seriously, I'm sure, and with Robert Rainwood it's a case of the legal mind sniffing out trouble where no trouble exists. Forget it."

He seemed so certain. Surely he wouldn't risk trouble with his wife. Perhaps Robert was mistaken, Bridget thought. It was hard to refuse Felix a helping hand when perhaps the whole future of the magazine was a stake.

"Could you sound her out, Felix? Tactfully, of course."

"My dear, if I detect so much as a whiff of resentment, I'll let you know and we'll think again. But I know Sue. There are no clouds in her sky. She thinks I'm a wonderful husband, and I think she's a delightful wife. My life away from this office is all hers. She knows that. Here, in my working life, you are a colleague. I'm not putting the clock back, Biddy. We can't be companions as before. But if we say we can't work together, we're admitting to an element that simply isn't there, and never was there. I need your help now. Would I ask if I thought I'd be injuring you or Sue?"

"No. I believe you, Felix. Robert must have drawn the wrong conclusion. I'll give you as much time as I can, but I'd like you to keep looking for an assistant at your price. And I don't want any salary. I'll be an honorary assistant as long as the emergency lasts."

"Bless you! I knew you wouldn't let me down. Three or four hours a day would suffice. That shouldn't give your father any cause for complaint."

"Just keep your ear to the ground, though, for any possible little rumblings from Susan."

"Of course. But there won't be."

"I must fly now, or I shall miss my bus."

"If you can hang on for quarter of an hour, I'll run you home. I'm leaving early tonight. Dinner with Sue's parents."

"No, I'll go for the bus, Felix, thanks all the same. Goodnight."

"Goodnight, Miss Armadale," he said solemnly.

When she had gone, he sat doodling on his pad for a few moments. Of course there was nothing in Rainwood's suggestions. If Sue laughingly referred to Bridget as his doting slave, she was only teasing, and inviting the punishment he meted out for such sauciness. He needed Bridget. She was good at the job, and he had to cut costs somehow if he was to meet Sue's bills. Besides, he liked having Biddy around. He was used to her, and saw no reason to lose her because of any fatheaded ideas of Robert Rainwood's. Sue excepted, he wasn't so sold on the Rainwoods.

Cycling along the lane towards Oakdene, the two back copies of The Monitor in the basket in front of her, Bridget rather hoped that Robert would not be at home. Those dark eyes of his could be disconcerting. She liked him, but was not prepared to have her inmost feelings dissected and regrouped in the way he thought advisable. She bent her head and cycled faster as she came to the white house with the green shutters on the outskirts of

Oakdene, and then wondered why. There was no reason why she should shrink from the house where Susan and Felix lived, to which she had not yet been invited.

The village of Oakdene consisted of no more than one row of shops set back from pavements edged with pollarded lime trees. On that sunny Saturday afternoon the shops, still closed for the lunch-hour, wore a sleepy air like the black cat sitting outside the newsagents, paws neatly tucked under, yellow eyes half-closed against the sun. Robert's house was on the far side of Oakdene, just past the cricket green where a few white-flannelled figures were now assembling. It was a pleasant, solid-looking house set well back from the lane behind a screen of silver birch trees which cast a dappled pattern across the lawn and the drive. The housekeeper was snipping off dead violas from the bed by the porch, and when Bridget explained her mission and proffered the magazines, she gave her a friendly smile and said:

"You'll find him just finishing his coffee in the garden. Won't you go round?"

And at that moment, Robert appeared round the side of the house, clad in grey slacks, jacketless, and with the sleeves of his white shirt rolled up in workmanlike fashion. He smiled and saluted her when he saw her, and refused to let her depart after she had explained her reason for calling. Before she quite knew how it had come about, her bicycle had been put round the side of the house and she had been put in a deck-chair on the terrace with a long, cold drink in her hand.

"Too hot for work," he said, stretching his long legs before him and tilting the shade of his deck-chair to a more useful angle. "Meilie's a glutton for gardening and puts me to shame."

"I like it, too. Don't you?"

"Well enough. Thanks for the magazines. Has Felix found a new assistant editor yet?"

"Not yet."

"He understood your reasons for not taking it on, I'm sure."

"Not really. He thought you'd taken it all too seriously. That Susan was only joking."

He turned and looked at her then, and feeling very much the toad beneath the harrow, Bridget turned her attention to Miss Mellon's excellent home-made lemon barley drink.

"And so?" asked Robert.

"And so what?"

"Are you doing the job?"

"Until Felix can find a replacement."

"I see."

Under his eyes, she felt forced to explain.

"Felix is in a spot. He can't afford to pay a high salary. I must see him through until he can find the right person at the right price."

"Did he persuade you, or didn't you need any persuading?"

"We discussed it sensibly," said Bridget coldly, nettled by his dry tone, "and since Felix is the best person to know how Susan feels, I accepted his word that it will not trouble her at all if I work there as a part-time assistant until a successor is found."

"I'd say that wishful thinking played a big part in your sensible discussion. However, it's your funeral. I think you're being very foolish and refusing to face unpleasant facts. Your stepfather was right about the Armadale constancy."

"I'll go now. Thank you for the drink," said Bridget, her cheeks flushed as she stood up.

"Don't be silly," he said, catching her arm. "You're as prickly as a hedgehog. You asked me that night to help you. I know you must have been feeling desperate to make such an appeal, since you're an independent young madam, but you need friends, Bridget, and I'd like to help. It will only be on the basis of straight talk, though. I can't wrap things up, and to utter soothing noises as though you're a child would be of no service to you, anyway. If you can accept an honest-to-God basis, say so, and sit down again. If you can't, all right. Go off in a state of huffiness and I'll not meddle any more. It's up to you. Which is it to be?"

She looked down at him, struggling with herself. He was right. She did need friends. The gap that Felix had left in her life was so enormous that she had been reduced to a state of cold inertia lately that was worse than the wild desolation that had first overtaken her. Life with her stepfather was so bleak without Felix to companion her leisure hours that she often felt as though life was being squeezed out of her, that she was becoming a mummy. And there was something about Robert, for all his irritating calm assumption of authority, that was tremendously reassuring. She felt his strength like a rock to lean on. She stood there, studying his face gravely, her little spurt of anger gone. Then she sat down, gave him a crooked little smile and said:

"I'll learn to take it, I expect. Be patient with me. I've one skin less than I could do with just now."

"The top one has probably been delicately hacked to little pieces by Uncle Owen. We'll leave the prickly matter of Felix Parvey for the time being, since you've decided to accept his word against mine, but tell me, Bridget, is your stepfather always as uncharitable to you as he appeared the other night? I was horrified by his attitude. I hadn't dreamed things were as bad as that."

"I've always hoped they would get better. I've tried. And sometimes I've felt that if only I had a different name, we could meet on terms of respect, if nothing else. When we talk about my work, for instance, he forgets and seems to treat me as an equal. Then it evaporates, and we're back in hostile country again."

"Sniping is a particularly mean form of hostility."

"He was tired that night. We have long spells when formal politeness is the routine. Or silence. Our meals are usually silent, and I really see very little of him apart from mealtimes. He works in his study, and has no leisure himself."

"A happy atmosphere, I must say."

"It didn't seem to matter so much when Felix . . ."

"Quite."

"It could be worse. I feel disloyal, talking about him like this. He has always been generous with money, given me anything I've wanted. In a cold sort of way, he does his duty towards me, you know, and expects me to do the same."

"Duty! Cold comfort. I can't think of a worse atmosphere myself, if what I witnessed was typical."

"He could be brutal, but he's never that. Always polite, icily polite. I've learned not to show my feelings. What hurts more than anything is my failure to understand him, to generate any warmth at all between us, because at odd moments, in a way I can't explain, I feel sorry for him. But I make no progress. I know I'm not his child, but am I as displeasing as all that? I've always tried to please him, never caused him trouble. What is there about me that he dislikes so much?"

So she knew nothing of the past, thought Robert, ferreting in the pockets of the sports jacket hanging on his chair and taking out his pipe. It seemed to him that she ought to know, if only to wipe away the sense of guilt that she seemed to feel because she was unloved. But he hesitated, not being a man given to gossip, and knowing from experience that things were seldom coloured clearly black or white, and that he was not in a position to judge the past of an older generation from facts given him at second-hand. He compromised, saying:

"Uncle Owen seems to take a misanthropic view of everybody. He hasn't a good word to say for any of the family. To explain that calls for a psychiatrist and a knowledge of the past that we don't have. As a family, though, we don't run to misanthropes, unless you count Great-Uncle Arthur, and he's not exactly a misanthrope, he's a catharsis."

"I used to be terrified of Uncle Arthur when I was a child. He was the ogre of all my books. I don't really know any of the Rainwoods well, though, except Grandma. Since Mother died, I've lost touch, and the cousins have all grown up in the meantime."

"Well, you must renew acquaintance with Kit when she's home for the summer vacation. She's not a bad representative of the

98

generation. I think you might get on well with her."

"I remember her being fished out of the pond at Grandma's once, covered in green slimy weed. She'd fallen in trying to get a better view of a frog, and once in, she couldn't see any reason for coming out until she'd seen all she wanted. I thought it was very logical at the time, but Mother was horrified and Grandma very stern. The smell of that weed was horrible. I've never forgotten it."

"I can't guarantee that the same logic doesn't work towards the same disastrous conclusions even now," said Robert, smiling, "but she seems to emerge with undimmed enthusiasm."

"What is her ambition?"

"To go plant-hunting in the Himalayas or on a permanent safari to South Africa studying wild animals, as far as I can gather. A science degree is her immediate objective, though."

"Either way, it seems to add up to an interesting life. Perhaps she'd let me go along with her as a kind of Boswell, writing up her adventures. That would be fun."

"My young sister will have to come down

to earth and put in some solid work on a more mundane level before she realises any of these exotic dreams."

"Good to have dreams, though."

"Have you any?"

"Not just now. My imagination is a bit bogged down."

"Only temporarily, then. Those articles suggest a person of quite vivid imagination. You bring the past to life, taking a little romantic licence here and there, though."

"Which your devotion to facts deplores?"

"No. You play fair and make it clear which is fact and which your imagination."

It was pleasant, sitting there in the garden, chatting. Bridget found him an intelligent, easy companion when he wasn't directing her life. The air was heavy with the scent of the old-fashioned pinks blooming in the borders, and there was a constant hum of bees about the catmint that grew at the edge of the terrace.

"Your home always had a happy feeling about it," she said suddenly after a pause. "Your mother loved the garden, I remember."

"Yes."

"It had an ambience of warmth and

security. I didn't analyse it like that at the time, of course, but when I remember our visits, it's always this garden I see in the sunshine. I'm glad you stayed on here, although perhaps it was a painful decision."

"I wanted Kit to have a base. At eighteen, it's hard to have your world shattered. And we're both fond of the place. Fortunately, Miss Mellon has proved a gem and has fitted in with us as though made for the part."

"How did you find her?"

"Need you ask? Grandma. Miss Mellon had nursed an invalid father for most of her life. He died and she was left with very little money. She was glad to take on the job. Grandma had visited her father for years. They lived in Melbridge."

"I think Grandma would always know someone to meet any emergency."

"Comes of living in the same place for so many years, and having a social conscience. There have been Rainwoods in Melbridge for several generations now."

She stayed to have tea with him, and had been lulled by his company and the pleasures of a garden on a warm June afternoon into a state of tranquillity when, walking with her to the gate, he had to shatter it by saying:

"Goodbye, Bridget. Thanks again for the magazines. But quit The Monitor quickly if you want to keep out of trouble."

7

GOSSIP

IT was early in July when Bridget had the first intimation of trouble, and it came from her stepfather. At dinner that evening he was as cold and uncommunicative as usual, until she brought in the coffee, when he said:

"Unfortunately, I found myself in the same railway carriage as Uncle Peter this evening. He seems to regard your association with Felix as highly undesirable and asked me if I would remind you that Felix is a married man and that it's time you realised that fact."

Bridget turned scarlet and her eyes flashed angrily as she said:

"I hope you told him that I'm only helping Felix out until he can find a new assistant editor, and that our association is purely a business one."

"I told him that I had no information on the matter but that I would pass his comment on."

"What beastly minds people have! You know I never see Felix outside of office hours now, and this is only a temporary arrangement. You could have told Uncle Peter."

"My dear girl, I had no wish to embark on a long argument with my brother, whose pompous waffling I find very irritating. I wanted to finish reading The Times. I pass his message on as a warning. I would rather you did not get yourself talked about in this connection."

"How can I help it if people are so malicious?"

"By cutting off your association with Felix, of course. But that would be too painful to you, no doubt."

She looked at his cold face incredulously.

"You think I'm forgetting that Felix is married?"

"Hardly. But you're seeking what consolation you can, perhaps."

"How can you say that? You must know me better than that."

"Don't let us have childish heroics. I know that you were in love with Felix Parvey, and constancy, as I've reminded you before, runs in your blood."

"As soon as Felix has found an assistant, I

shall be leaving The Monitor for good," said Bridget, cut by his irony.

"It's taking him a long time. Is he trying hard, do you think?"

"It's difficult to find journalists out of London."

"Too bad. Well, I've some work to do. I shall not be drawn into any family squabbles, Bridget. You're of an age to manage your own affairs, and I take no sides. However, I advise discretion, and I repeat that it would be distastful to have you at the centre of a family scandal."

He left her then. He took no sides, she thought bitterly. Surely she was entitled to his loyalty, if not his affection. But this news forced her hand. She had been uneasy for the last week or two at Felix's apparent lack of success in finding a successor to Jim Travers, and she had no evidence that he had been really trying. He must have been wrong in saying that Susan had no objection to the present arrangement, for nothing else could account for Uncle Peter's remarks. Dismayed, she wished she had been firmer about a time limit to her offer, and wondered just how far this talk among the family had gone. While she was wondering, however, Mirabel

Rainwood was taking steps to stop it . . .

In the drawing-room at Bredon Lodge on that same sultry July evening, Susan crossed her pretty legs, leaned back in the armchair and gave her grandmother a charming smile as she said:

"Well, here I am, Grandma, in answer to your summons. It was a little mysterious, being asked to come alone. Felix is working tonight, though, so he didn't mind."

"As you know, Susan, I am not a person to beat about the bush. There is a whispering campaign going on among the family discrediting Bridget, hinting that she is trying to take Felix from you."

Susan's brown eyes opened wide.

"Is there? Felix and I have no worries, Grandma."

"Perhaps not. But I won't have Bridget's name bandied about like this and I'm going to get to the bottom of it. Who started these rumours, Susan? You?"

"Of course not."

"I shall ask all round the family. I thought it better to start with you, since you're the person most concerned. Perhaps I should have asked Felix to come along, too."

"No, don't drag Felix into this, Grandma."

106

"Why not? Bridget was his friend. He'll not like to have gossip of this sort about her, especially as he's liable to suffer from it himself."

"Oh, everybody knows it's no fault of Felix's," said Susan quickly. "She's always clung to him like a vine."

Mirabel's face grew more stern.

"So you *have* been talking about her."

"I've said nothing that isn't common knowledge and has been for months. I can't be blamed if the relatives gossip and take seriously what I regard as a bit of a joke."

"I'm sure you're not as heartless as that makes you sound, Susan. And I can't help thinking that Felix would be shocked to know that you are making trouble for a girl who was for many years a good friend."

"But really, Grandma," said Susan, changing her tactics, "I'm not making any trouble. I can't help it if Bridget spends more time at The Monitor office than ever before and people draw their own conclusions."

"I understand from Robert that Felix was in some difficulty over replacing an assistant and that he'd asked Bridget to help out until he'd found someone."

Susan shrugged her shoulders.

"That's her story. She suggested it, I've no doubt. She's not being paid, you know. She's doing it for love," concluded Susan with a tight little smile that betrayed a lot to her grandmother.

"Then I'm afraid I shall have to see Felix, and get an explanation."

"No, don't do that, Grandma. I don't want him worried. There's no need. I'm quite sure of Felix."

"Then what do you want, Susan? To blacken Bridget's name?"

"If the cap fits, it's no fault of mine. Perhaps when she realises that people recognise her game, she'll give it up. If not . . ."

"If not?"

"Then I shall suggest to Felix that he gives up The Monitor. It's not a good enough job for a person of his talents, anyway."

And there speaks her father, thought Mirabel, dismayed at the vindictiveness behind her grand-daughter's words, but aware that jealousy was cruel, and that Susan must be afraid of Bridget's hold on Felix's affection and see it as a threat to her marriage, however unjustified her fears might be. She was young, spoilt, and very much in love with her husband, and she knew how long-

108

standing his friendship with Bridget had been.

"Now listen to me, dear," said Mirabel more gently. "You can be forgiven for wanting to protect your marriage, even if the threat is imaginary, as I'm sure it is. I know Bridget. You don't. When I tell her what is being said, I know she will immediately leave The Monitor although it will inconvenience Felix."

"Will she?" said Susan eagerly.

"I can guarantee that. In return, I look to you to rebuke any talk about Bridget, which must reflect on Felix as well, remember. You have so much to make you happy, dear. A devoted husband, a delightful home. To allow gossip like this can damage not only Bridget, but all of you, and it's completely unfounded. You have my word for that, and you know me well enough not to doubt my word."

"Of course, Grandma."

"It's a bargain, then?"

"Yes."

"I'm glad I haven't had to bring Felix into this. He's a sensitive boy. He would find it all very distasteful."

"Quite," said Susan, shrewd enough to get the warning.

"I'll have a word with Bridget tomorrow. She's been too good-natured in helping Felix out. People can be very uncharitable in judging other people's motives."

"Well, it's the middle-aged people who like gossiping," said Susan with a little smile.

"Then you can enjoy feeling virtuous by putting them in the wrong, dear."

After Susan had driven off in the smart little car her father had given her on her last birthday, Mirabel telephoned Bridget, who promised to come over the next evening.

"Was that young Susan's car I saw shooting off just now?" inquired Charles Rainwood, coming in from the garden.

"Yes, dear."

"No time to come and say 'Good evening' to her grandfather."

"She was anxious to get back before dark because her rear light is defective."

"No manners. Always dashing about. What did she want, anyway?"

"I asked her to call to discuss some family gossip about Bridget which I didn't much like."

"H'm. Disposed of it?" he asked, his bushy eyebrows raised as he looked at his wife.

"I think so."

"Good. Susan's greedy, you know, Mirrie. Like Peter. Acquisitive streak in the family there. Odd, because it's not characteristic of the Rainwoods. Be better off now if some of us had a bit more of it, I suppose."

"It's probably my French ancestors who are responsible," said Mirabel, smiling. "My maternal grandmother was reputed to be a very grasping woman."

"It's your French blood that makes you manage this family so well, my dear. Puts the steel in the structure. Never decry it. Do you think we can run to a pump for this rock garden I'm planning? Be much more interesting to have a stream circulating. This is my idea. Look, I've mapped it out here."

He unrolled a sheet of graph paper with a plan of the proposed rock garden drawn with the meticulous detail at which he excelled, and Mirabel turned her attention to yet another family problem, the weighing of her husband's ambitious gardening plans against the slender means at their disposal.

That evening, she wrote in her diary:

Much dismayed at the gossip going round the family about Felix and Bridget. Started by Susan, I'm afraid, and fostered by Peter. There is a lack of sensitivity in Peter and his daughter which I find very trying, and which must surely jeopardise their personal relationships with others of less coarse fibre. I think I have stopped Susan from making more mischief, but I must have a serious talk with Bridget. I can't allow this sort of scandal in the family. Knowing Bridget, I am sure it is unjustified. Whatever her feeling for Felix, and I know she was very devoted to him, she would never try to come between him and his wife. She is, however, in some ways a very innocent child. Her life has been too secluded. But she must instil some ruthlessness into her dealings with Felix, who is obviously not without blame in allowing this sort of situation to arise.

It can, of course, be dangerous to interfere. I lost Owen by doing so. But I cannot stand aside when I see what ought to be done and others don't. My children would say that I sat in judgment too much. They would be quite right. It is an indulgence of old age which I have no intention of giving up.

8

PARTING OF THE WAYS

"WHO else but Susan could be behind Uncle Peter's remarks to Father?" asked Bridget quietly.

Felix drummed on his desk with his fingers, frowning, and said irritably:

"Sue's father is as fussy as an old hen where she's concerned. Seems to think I'm not capable of looking after her. He's puffing up some light-hearted remark of Sue's as Robert did. The Rainwoods seem addicted to petty gossip."

"But I don't care to be the subject of light-hearted remarks, as you put it," said Bridget, with a flash of temper.

Felix stood up then and put an arm round her shoulders in the old friendly fashion.

"Sorry, Biddy. It is beastly for you. I quite understand. But must you walk out on me? It'll all die down if we ignore it. I can vouch for Sue. She's not at the bottom of this, even

113

if her sense of humour is out of place. I'll ask her to pipe down on that."

"I'm sorry, Felix. It's gone too far. I'll work this week out. That's all. I shan't come again, and I think we'd better not see each other any more, except at family gatherings."

"Oh, this is absurd, Biddy. I need you. I simply can't afford to take on more staff. Being married is an expensive indulgence, I can tell you."

"It was your choice, Felix. I'm sorry. You know I'd be happy to work on here for The Monitor, but gossip makes that impossible now. Grandma Rainwood has asked me to see her tonight. I know what it's about."

"It's your life. Why let the Rainwoods boss you around?"

"I don't. But if you don't care what sort of a reputation I shall have if I stay on, I do."

"My dear, I'm sorry. Knowing you, it's inconceivable to me that anybody can talk about you like this."

"My mind's made up, Felix. I shall be leaving you at the end of this week."

"You'll keep in touch, though. Come in on Mondays with your column."

"I'll post the next four to give you time to make other arrangements to fill my space."

"Oh, confound it all! It's so stupid."

"No. I should have realised from the beginning that it wouldn't work. You haven't been married long, Felix, and you're happy, aren't you?"

"Yes."

"And whether it's absurd or not, this talk could spoil your happiness, make trouble between you and Susan. I know you believe that she has nothing to do with the gossip, but whether she has or not, the fact that there is gossip could destroy her confidence in you. For your sake, as well as mine, we must end our partnership."

"But it's innocent enough. We both know that. Hang it all, I've known you for more than ten years."

"You can't expect marriage not to change things. Let's be glad about the ten years, and leave it at that. You've so many compensations, Felix."

"Must you really go, Biddy?"

It was hard to resist the appeal in his eyes, but she said firmly:

"Yes, really, Felix."

"All right, my dear. And thank you for all you've done."

The telephone saved her from replying,

and she slipped out of his office, tears pricking her eyes.

The threatening storm of the past two days broke that afternoon, and Bridget arrived home soaked after the walk from the bus stop. Her grandmother telephoned her to say that as Robert was coming to discuss some business matters with his grandfather, she had asked him to pick Bridget up on his way. He arrived earlier than she had expected.

"Can you just give me five minutes?" she asked. "I must finish re-typing an article tonight. Only half a page to do."

"Sure," he said, as thunder ripped across the sky above them and the rain fell as though hurled down by a giant.

Bridget winced as lightning zig-zagged across the window, and said:

"I hate storms. I can't concentrate on anything. I've already had two goes to re-type this last page."

"Can I help? Read it out to you?"

"No, thanks. I think I'll manage best on my own, but if you could use your strength to close my study window, I'd be grateful. The rain's coming through in a little stream, and I never can close it tightly. The metal frame's warped."

"Right. I'll have a look at it. Uncle Owen not in?"

"No. He's working late at the office tonight."

In her study, Robert investigated the window-frame, removed the sodden bits of newspaper with which she had ineffectually tried to stem the leaks, and after two attempts, managed to close the window tightly and push home the catch.

"Strong man. Thank you very much," said Bridget, mopping up the pool on the floor with a cloth. "Would you like to wait for me in the sitting-room? More comfortable there."

"This looks snug enough to me," said Robert, sitting down in the old rocking-chair. "Carry on."

Bridget went on typing, rather wishing he had left her alone. He was not the sort of person whose presence she could ignore and she wanted all her concentration to finish her task quickly. With an effort, she pulled her mind back to the description of the branch public library recently opened in Lynwood village, with which she was concluding her weekly column for The Monitor.

Robert sat back and looked around him

117

with some interest. It was the first time he had been in this downstairs room at the back of the house. It was pleasantly furnished: a low coffee-table beside his rocking-chair, chintz cushions in the little alcoves each side of the fireplace, a portable radio set on one of the alcove seats, a book-case, and a corner cupboard with a bowl of nasturtiums on it. Her desk was a large, old-fashioned one, and on it was a brass turn-up calendar and a pretty little brass clock. A folder, a few sheets of typescript, a dictionary and her portable typewriter utilised most of the remaining surface. There were no pictures on the cream walls, and only one photograph on the book-case. The plain carpet was the colour of beech-leaves in autumn and the design on the chintz curtains was of autumn leaves tumbling over a cream background. The whole effect was warm and intimate in contrast to the rest of the house, which was handsomely furnished in an austere way and seemed to reflect Uncle Owen's cold personality. The desk and the typewriter in no way impinged on the feminine cosiness of the room. This was her world, thought Robert, away from her stepfather. Here was her retreat. Her sanctuary in this cold, hostile house.

She left him for a few minutes while she tidied herself, and he moved across to the book-case. The photograph was of Felix, leaning on a little stone bridge across a stream. The detail was not very sharp and it was evidently an enlargement from a snapshot, but the composition was good, with Felix smiling from a patch of sunlight, the bridge in dappled shade from a tree. He replaced the photograph and inspected the books: a complete set of Jane Austen, some poetry anthologies, two very old Harrison Ainsworth historical romances, a biography of Dickens, Fowler's Modern English Usage, a few country and travel books, and a small group of well-known children's books including Little Women and The Wind in the Willows. He moved back to his chair and picked up the book lying on the coffee-table. It was another anthology of poetry, and as he opened it at the book-mark, he found himself looking at Shakespeare's sonnet:

When to the sessions of sweet silent
  thought
I summon up remembrance of things
  past . . .

On the fly-leaf was written, "To my dear Biddy. Felix. Christmas, 1964". He closed the book with an impatient bang and returned it to its resting-place as Bridget came in.

"I think the storm's moving away," she said. "I'm sorry to have held you up, Robert."

"There was no hurry. I like your private haven, Bridget. I'm privileged to have been allowed in, I guess."

"I'm attached to it. I feel . . . safe in here."

"I understand. But don't shut yourself up in an ivory tower yet awhile. You're too young."

In the car, she sat pale and silent beside him while the rain pelted down so that the windscreen wipers could scarcely cope with the torrent. The car wheels sent up showers of spray and the lanes were awash.

"Why does this always happen when the roses are at their best?" asked Bridget when they turned into the drive of Bredon Lodge and saw the bed of roses almost flattened by the barrage, rose petals strewn in the mud. "I sometimes think nature has a grudge against the world. All that beauty, wasted."

She jumped as another peal of thunder

crashed overhead, and lightning seemed to stab the neighbouring field. The storm had come back in full force and now seemed to be right over them. Robert took her hand and she held his tightly for a moment, giving him a wan smile.

"I'm a fool about storms."

"We all have our bogeys."

"Do you? I can't imagine you being frightened of anything."

"Operations. My blood runs cold when I think of surgery."

"But you wouldn't know anything about it."

"That's the trouble. I'd be in a cold sweat beforehand, thinking what those surgeons might do while I was powerless to stop them."

"That seems to argue lack of faith in surgeons more than cowardice."

"You have a point there," he said, smiling. "I have the Rainwood suspicion of scientific experts. What are you being hauled up before the bench for? Or is this purely a social call?"

"Grandma didn't say specifically, but I know. Haven't you heard the gossip going around about Felix and me?"

"I haven't had any contact with the family

121

for the past few weeks. What's the latest?"

She told him and he said:

"Grandma won't stand for this sort of trouble in the family. Why have you let it tag on like this, Bridget? I did warn you."

"I know. Felix hasn't been able to find anybody to take on the job."

"Has he tried?"

"I don't know. I assumed so."

"You should have made it your business to know. I confess I'm still not sure where you stand in all this. Are you really so ingenuous that you didn't expect this? Or are you ready to take the risk of serious trouble just to keep in touch with Felix? What is the truth?"

"I told you before. I've stayed on only because Felix was in a hole and asked me to hold on until he'd found somebody."

"And now?"

"I'm leaving at the end of this week."

"Is that definite?"

"Yes. I'm not seeing him again after that. I made it quite plain."

"He shouldn't have left it to you, or have made use of you like this."

"We've been friends for many years. You can ask things of friends. I don't blame Felix."

122

"Of course not," said Robert dryly.

"And I'm sick and tired of having my feelings raked over by all and sundry. It started with Felix's engagement and I've never been allowed the decent privacy anybody is entitled to. How would you like your personal affairs discussed by the whole of the Rainwood family? Would you enjoy being advised and lectured and told what you should feel?"

"I shouldn't have allowed myself to be put in that position," said Robert calmly. "My private feelings would have remained private, but if I'd been passed over by my girl for someone else, I shouldn't have hung around waiting for any crumbs she cared to toss me. That would have invited comment."

"Oh, Mr. Know-all," said Bridget, exasperated. "You've got everything so neatly docketed. Analysis is so easy when you're a looker-on, but feelings aren't so easily docketed."

"I never said they were. It's a case of not letting your heart rule your head, as you've been doing."

"Everybody is so anxious to tell me what my heart and my head should do. You all know so much more about it than I do. If the Rainwoods would look after their own affairs and not poke their noses into other people's, this whole beastly business would have been avoided. It's other people who have blown this up into something false. It's not Felix's fault or mine. Felix made a simple appeal to a friend to help him out of a difficult position caused by Jim Travers leaving The Monitor. Because I answered that appeal, I've become the centre of a squalid campaign of spiteful gossip. It's contemptible."

"Well, now you've got that off your chest, remember one person you've left out. Felix's wife. Doesn't she come into it?"

"Felix says Susan has never bothered about it."

"Rubbish! Who else would have started this talk? I told you how she felt weeks ago. Felix is either a fool, or else he wants the best of both worlds: the privileges of a married man and the freedom of a single man. And Susan won't stand for that. And before you fly to the defence of Felix in a state of righteous anger, let me blow another hole in your attack. Whatever the motives of the rest of the Rainwoods, there are two of us who have only been concerned to spare you further unhappiness. Grandma has been thinking only of you, because she's very fond of you and knew what Felix meant in your life. I wanted to help you because you appealed for help on one occasion and because I thought you'd enough to put up with from your home life without asking for more trouble. I don't usually concern myself with other people's personal affairs, let alone those of a lovesick girl who seems quite incapable of logical processes of thought. In the cause of accuracy, you might exclude two Rainwoods, therefore, from the charge of poking their noses into your affairs and making trouble for you."

Listening to that deep, deliberate voice, Bridget's anger, which usually fell away as quickly as it rocketed up, was now replaced by a glimmering of humour. His dark blue eyes were looking at her with some severity, and her lips twitched as she said:

"You must be quite effective in court, Robert. Two Rainwoods are hereby removed from my indictment, and I agree that I overlooked Susan. You see, I can be logical sometimes."

"Practise hard, and it may become a habit."

"And I *am* grateful for your help. And after this week there will be no more contact with Felix."

"Then we have no quarrel. Are you going to be able to put him out of your heart, too?" he asked quietly, putting his hand on hers.

"I don't think I can. He's been there too long. And I don't even think I want to. Memories are a comfort and don't hurt anyone."

"But yourself. You're alone too much. He wouldn't loom so large if you'd had other companions."

"Perhaps not. But I can't change the pattern of my life."

"With any other girl, I'd take a bet that in a year's time, she'd be heartfree again, if not involved with a new claimant. But with you, Bridget, I'm not so sure," said Robert slowly, remembering the history of her mother.

"The storm's over. Look, the sun's just coming out from under that cloud."

Robert ignored this red herring and went on: "I can't help thinking that it would be a great pity and very foolish to make a little shrine to the past instead of putting it behind you."

"How would you start? You can't blot out ten years."

"I'd start by removing that photograph from your book-case," said Robert.

"Dear Robert," she said with a little smile. "Always so practical. If we don't present ourselves to Grandma, she'll think we've been involved in an accident."

When Robert disappeared into the study with his grandfather, Bridget turned to Grandma Rainwood and took the plunge directly.

"I know what you want to see me about, Grandma. All the gossip about Felix and me. I'm sorry. It's quite unfounded, but I'm leaving The Monitor office at the end of the week and I shan't be seeing Felix again. I just don't want to talk about it any more, though."

"And nor do I, dear. There's been enough unpleasantness. I just want you to know that I saw Susan about it last night. She will scotch any more gossip, provided you leave The Monitor. I told her that I knew you would do that, once you knew what was being said."

"It was Susan, then, who started it."

"I'm afraid so. You must make allowances, dear. She's only twenty, and very much in love with her husband. That doesn't excuse her, but makes it a little more understandable."

"Well, thank you for not doubting me."

"I know you, Bridget. As I knew your father and mother. There's no need to say any more about it. Now come and have a look at Grandpa's plan for a new rock garden. He can talk of nothing else and it really is a rather splendid conception."

And that was the end of the matter, although the ugliness and pain of it lingered on with Bridget for a long time. When Robert drove her home that night, he made no reference to it, and seemed rather withdrawn. Her stepfather's car drove in just ahead of them, and Bridget felt chilled at the prospect of going in. Her life, deprived completely now of the warmth of Felix's friendship, seemed set in a barren, cold country. She was reluctant to leave Robert's side. He was strong, dependable, with a human warmth that her life lacked. His judicial calm might irritate her sometimes, his insistence on facing facts might sometimes make him an uncomfortable companion, his authority might provoke her to rebel, but with him she felt alive. He offered the comfort of a fire at which to warm her cold hands. Impulsively, she put a hand on his arm as she said:

"Goodnight, Robert, and thank you for everything."

"Everything meaning what?" he asked quizzically. "Being an infernal nuisance?"

"Just for bothering," she said in a rather shaky voice as she slid out of the car.

9

LANDMARK

ON a Thursday morning a few weeks later, Robert telephoned Bridget to ask her if she would care to come to some kennels near Rushleigh to help him choose a Labrador puppy for his sister's birthday. She arranged to meet him the next evening at the stile opposite the church.

Sitting on the stile waiting for him, with the evening sun warm on her face, she reflected with mixed feelings on the party which Grandma Rainwood was giving the next evening to celebrate the twentieth birthday of Christine and her cousin, Nicholas Barbury, who had made family history by being born on the same day. After the events of the past weeks, she felt reluctant to face the family assembly to which she felt she had never really belonged. Then Robert turned the corner of the lane and she waved. She had not seen him since the day of the storm, and felt unexpectedly glad to see that rugged face.

He was the one person in her world just then with whom she could relax, be herself without any inhibitions, without any defences.

They set off along the old packhorse track between hedges bright with blackberry flowers and fragrant with honeysuckle.

"Does Christine know about this or is it a surprise?" asked Bridget.

"A surprise. She's wanted a dog ever since we lost our old Labrador a few years ago, but it didn't seem fair to saddle Miss Mellon with a dog when Kit would be away so much. However, Mellie has come round to the idea and says she'd be glad of the company if we'll do the exercising. Kit's not due home until tomorrow, so I thought I'd have the animal there to welcome her. I wasn't going to let her choose it herself, anyway. I know Kit. She'd come away with the sickliest looking one of the litter because she felt sorry for it."

Bridget couldn't hide her smile at this typically managerial attitude as she said:

"You know what points to look for, I expect. I doubt whether my judgment will be allowed to influence you. I shall be like Kit. Fall for a pair of soulful eyes."

"Ever thought of having a dog yourself?"

"Yes. But, much as I'd love one, I thought it best not to."

"Why?"

She hesitated, then said:

"Well, I suppose it sounds foolish, but I didn't want to give Father a handle he could use against me."

"How do you mean? Uncle Owen's a civilised person. He wouldn't ill-treat an animal."

"Oh no. I didn't mean that. It would all be much more subtle. I can't explain. But to make things tolerable, I have to present an absolutely smooth surface. Anything or any person I'm fond of gives him an opening. And he's such a perfectionist where his home is concerned that I know he'd find a dog just a noisy intrusion. I may be a coward, but I've learned to avoid trouble."

"Have you ever thought of leaving home? Striking out on your own?"

"Not until lately, when I've wondered. We don't seem to be very good for each other, Father and I. There's always a barrier between us. There's so much about him that I don't understand. But I do feel I owe him a duty. Mother was stranded with me, almost penniless, you know, when my father died.

My stepfather provided us with a comfortable home, gave us everything we wanted in a material way. Now I feel I must keep the home going for him. He works terribly hard, and when my mother was dying, she told me to do my best for him. Although, looking back, I don't think they were happy together, he was grief-stricken when she died. For weeks afterwards, he said scarcely a word. I'm afraid I've proved little consolation. If I'd been his own child, I suppose it might have been different."

"Perhaps. Family relationships are all very tricky. We understand too little of each other; the communication is often faulty. You're coming to the family party tomorrow, I take it."

"Yes. Father's not coming. He's too busy. I'm not sure that I'm exactly happy about coming, after all the gossip about me. And I've always felt a bit of an outsider, you know."

"That's silly. You're too thin-skinned. You come and enjoy yourself and show the flag. You'll bury the gossip far more effectively by joining in the party happily than by being conspicuous by your absence. It may comfort you to know that you're not the only one who views it with something short of enthusiasm. Kit is definitely not a party girl."

"Isn't she? That's surprising. She seems such a happy, confident girl."

"Oh, she's confident enough. Just bored with social functions, and very conscious of her grandmother's critical view of her social performance. Everything happens to Kit at a party. Clothes fall apart, stockings ladder, drinks get spilled, and her sense of humour usually falls foul of some unsympathetic spirit in the family. And she adores Great-Uncle Arthur!"

"She sounds refreshing."

"A fresh breeze is not always timely. Let's see what this place has to offer, and remember that soulful eyes are less important than a good temperament. Kit provides us with all the excitement we want."

From a litter of eight, Bridget found it difficult to choose, all but one being equally adorable. The exception was the largest, a masterful dog who trampled over his brothers and sisters with a callous insistence on monopolising the attention of the humans. This one, eventually, Robert chose.

"You've picked a good one there," said the owner of the kennels. "He'll train easily. The mother's been doing some training herself, and this fellow's led the class."

Without, it seemed, a pang of regret or uneasiness at leaving his family, the new acquisition romped about at their heels as they walked back. He was the colour of creamy coffee, with dark brown eyes and an exuberant but unsteady gait which had him tumbling down ditches and stumbling over hummocky grass. Unfeeling towards his family he might be, but Bridget found him a captivating companion as she encouraged him along and played with him. Robert watched him with amused detachment, as though summing up his potentialities.

"I think I'll cut across the heath home, Bridget. It'll save putting him on a lead. He'll be best trained to that in the garden. If you feel like the walk, come back with me and have a cup of coffee, and I'll drive you home."

And so they walked across the heath to Oakdene. In the mellow light of the setting sun, the heather took on a richer purple and the silver birch trees stood motionless in the calm evening air. The white sandy track they followed was soft to their feet, and the puppy began to tire. When they were nearly home,

135

he sat down with a little whine, his front legs straight and his rear askew, looking up at them, and Robert picked him up and carried him for the rest of the way.

Driving home along the lane with Robert that night, under a star-pricked sky with a feather of a moon, she said:

"This has been the happiest evening I've had for ages, Robert. Thank you for taking me along."

"A simple enough expedition."

"But happiness lies in simple things."

"True. We let life get a lot too complicated and sophisticated. If Kit wants a companion when she exercises the animal, are you willing?"

"More than willing."

"Right. I'll tell her."

It took only a few minutes to drive from Oakdene to her home in Rushleigh. After Robert had left her, she leaned on the gate, enjoying the beauty of that summer night. The trees along the lane were heavy in leaf, dark, brooding shapes, and the spicy scent of a balsam poplar hung on the air. Happiness had been a stranger to her for so long now that she wanted to hug it closely to her, to linger with it. Once indoors it would evaporate like dew in a desert. It was odd that when Felix went from her, he had taken, too, her old delight in the simple things of nature. It was as though she had become blind and insensitive to its beauty. That evening, some of the old delight had returned, and with it, a sense of healing.

Whether or not Grandma Rainwood had briefed Susan beforehand, she was charming and friendly to Bridget at the party. Felix looked tired, but told Bridget that he was coping quite well without a sub-editor. She had no difficulty in keeping their contacts scarce without seeming to be deliberately avoiding him, for the Rainwoods were present in full force that evening, and with the addition of a few young friends of the grandchildren, the party mustered thirty.

The first half of the evening limped a little. The generations tended to hive off into conclaves. There was a little desultory dancing among the young Rainwoods, but the party seemed to suffer from lack of participation of the two principal players. Nicholas, a slight, handsome boy with long, fair hair, one lock of which fell poetically over his forehead, the classical features of his grandmother, and an affected, languid manner which that lady would have scorned, spent most of the time leaning on the grand piano looking ineffably bored. Christine, lively and voluble for the first half-hour, then vanished and was not seen again until it was nearly supper-time, when she edged cautiously back into the drawing-room in the wake of Great-Uncle Arthur, looking a little guilty. Avoiding her grandmother's eyes, she slipped across the room to Bridget while her great-uncle made a bee-line for Grandma Rainwood, his booming voice surmounting the dance music like a drum accompaniment. Bridget rather suspected this diversion to have been pre-arranged.

"Hullo," said Christine, smiling. "Robert tells me you helped him to choose my beautiful Boris."

"That is an overstatement. I went along and was instructed on the points to note while Robert made the choice."

"Well, that's what I meant," said Christine, grinning. "He's a darling. Boris, I mean."

"Yes. Boris is a good name for him."

"I chose it because he reminds me of one of our Profs of that name. They have the same

'Please-like-me' appeal and the same cajoling eyes."

"Sounds like a dangerous Professor."

"Not really. He's lamb all through. No wolf. How's the party going?"

"I don't think it's really got off the ground yet."

"Parties never do, for me. But I've just had a jolly hour playing snooker with Uncle Arthur. He's wizard at it. I'm not bad. I'm going to get a black mark from Grandma, though."

"Could be. But at least you've been enjoying yourself. Your cousin looks as though he's loathing every minute."

"Oh, Nick's an effete ass. Thinks we're all Philistines, and is too superior for words. He might try to look interested. After all, Grandma thinks she is doing us a kindness."

Bridget's laugh rang out at this kind condescension and her eyes danced as she said:

"Robert was right. You do bring a fresh breeze."

"Oh, I'm a social misfit. I know that," said Christine, her quirky little face expressing no evidence of regret. "And I simply loathe dressing up in formal clothes. These shoes are killing me. But Grandma expects it.

Bredon Lodge has its standards. You're all right. You're obviously the sort of person that clothes like. They hate me."

"Well, killing shoes or not, I think your cousin is going to ask you to dance."

But it was Bridget whom Nicholas approached. With a slight bow and a cool, appraising eye, he said with a drawl:

"Would you care to dance? Grandma seems to think it's fitting to wind up the dancing with a waltz before we eat. She thinks that's the sort of dance we still do."

Christine gave Bridget a wink as they moved off. Young Nicholas was quite a competent partner, and at supper afterwards, calmly changing the names carefully placed in order round the dining-table, he sat next to her and talked about John Ruskin and Proust, practically ignoring the rest of the party. The fact that she wrote, and actually had her writing published, although only in obscure publications, seemed to have marked her out as the sole person present to whom he considered he would be intelligible. Bridget enjoyed him, and thought that time would probably rub off the more preposterous aspects of this young aesthete and reveal an attractive personality.

"How the aunts and uncles love a party!" he said, towards the end of an excellent meal. "They're really period pieces, you know, the Rainwoods. In spirit, they belong to the good old vicarage days of Grandfather's youth. His father was in the church, you know."

"And what were the vicarage days like?" asked Bridget wickedly.

"I get the picture from Mother, who spent holidays there when she was a kid. She's the nostalgic type. Loves talking about it. You know. Tennis or croquet on the lawn, cucumber sandwiches under the beech tree. All terribly nice."

"Well, you can't call Great-Aunt Lucille a vicarage type," said Bridget, looking down the table as a peal of laughter came from a smartly-dressed woman with a rather heavily made-up face, tight white curls, and pendant diamond earrings which flashed with every movement and teamed up with the richly jewelled rings on the hands which she used so eloquently as she talked.

"Ah, she's not a Rainwood. She belongs to Grandma's side of the family, and there's a French strain there. I must say I rather go for Aunt Lucille, though she's devoted her life to the squalid business of making money. She's a change from the rest. Picturesque. Extravagant. She's made a fortune out of the beauty business, you know."

"Has she? I've only seen her once before. She's certainly a break from the old tradition."

"Her visits are rare. She's abroad a lot. Descends on us like a prima donna visiting the Women's Institute. Good grief! Grandpa's never going to make a speech, is he?"

Charles Rainwood's speech was brief, but his kind reference to the two grandchildren whose birthday they were celebrating merely sent Nicholas's eyebrows shooting heavenwards, as though this, in all conscience, was more than any man ought to have to bear, while Christine studied the bowl of roses in front of her with deep concentration.

Nicholas waved a languid hand in acknowledgment and Christine smiled apologetically as the family drank their health.

"I have an awful feeling that we're going to be dragged into playing frightful games after this," murmured Nicholas darkly.

And indeed, he was right, for his mother and Great-Aunt Lucille announced that they were going to pick teams for charades, and Nicholas's incredulous expression at this proposed juvenility brought the glint of laughter to Bridget's eyes again. However, Lucille proved as expert at organising charades as she was at organising her beauty salons, and her second choice for a career might well have been the stage, for she proved a colourful and skilled actress and whipped up her team to unsuspected displays of talent, even the long-suffering Nicholas proving a very passable Romeo to Susan's Juliet. And somehow, after that release of inhibitions, the party went with a swing, ending up with a polka started off by Great-Aunt Lucille and Great-Uncle Arthur. Bridget, skipping round the room happily with Nicholas, felt as light-hearted as she was light-footed. The world seemed a different place at Bredon Lodge that evening. Robert was right, she thought. She had become too shut off from life. Now, she felt the horizon widening.

Robert drove her home. Christine waved her to the front seat of the car and settled herself in the back, saying, with a contented sigh:

"Well, that's that. It wasn't so bad, really."

"Then don't make such a fuss next time," said Robert.

"I really don't see why I shouldn't spend my own birthday as I like."

"You can't avoid certain social duties in this life, my girl. And you've not had a bad birthday."

"I know. It's been a jolly good one. Can't wait to get back to Boris, though. Would you like to come for a walk with Boris and me tomorrow afternoon, Bridget?"

"Love to."

"I'll drop you off, Kit, and you can take that animal round the garden before I get back."

"Righto."

When they were alone, Robert said:

"From all the evidence, I'd say you really enjoyed the party."

"I did. Haven't felt so light-hearted for years. In spite of young Nicholas's somewhat dim view of the Rainwood clan, I think they're an interesting mixture, and I wish I'd seen more of them in the past."

"There's time enough. It didn't bother you, seeing Felix and Susan?"

"No. I wasn't with them much, anyway." The only small pang, she thought, had been when she saw them leave together.

"Any backwash from Susan?"

"None. She was very charming."

"You seem to have made a hit with young Nick."

"Not a hit. I offered the best he could make of a very bad job. I found him most amusing."

"He's all right. At the age to enjoy posing."

"Did *you* enjoy the party? I didn't seem to see you around much. I believe you're as bad as Christine when it comes to taking evasive action."

"Well, I did have a quiet session in the study with Great-Uncle James. Haven't seen the old boy for ages. He was finding the noise a bit much."

"Let me see, he's Grandma Rainwood's brother, isn't he? Looks a dear, though I've hardly spoken to him."

"He's a little shy with young people. Shares a house in Sussex with Aunt Lucille. A great naturalist."

"They're not very alike, Grandma, her brother and her sister, are they?"

"Temperamentally, miles apart. That's a pretty frock you're wearing."

"Thank you. I'm sorry you forsook us for so long this evening. I'd have liked to see you dance the polka, Robert."

"I came in halfway through, in time to see you performing very nicely. I doubt whether I'd have been such a nimble partner as Nick."

"Such frivolous occupations don't appeal, perhaps."

"You're in a naughty mood."

"The frivolity's gone to my head. I'm not used to it."

"It suits you. I recommend a course of it as a cure for love."

"Will you be joining the walking party tomorrow afternoon?"

"Afraid not. I've some work to do."

"Don't you ever let up?"

"When I can."

"I think a course of frivolity might be good for you, too, Robert. The past two years have been unhappy and burdensome ones, I'm sure. I remember your family as such a happy and united one."

"Yes. Having it sliced in half was a savage blow. Worst for Kit, perhaps. I've had work to fill my mind and my days."

"But now you've earned some play-time."

"I don't think I'm exactly a playful person, but I'm open to conviction, of course," he said solemnly.

"I'll see what I can think up to lighten our burdens," said Bridget, half laughing.

He had stopped the car outside her house and switched on the inside light as she searched for her handbag. He found it between the seats, a small black silk bag embroidered with green and gold thread.

"How about payment for this, to start with?" he asked, holding it up.

Her grey eyes met his for a moment, shy and a little startled. Then her cheeks dimpled as she smiled and kissed him quickly, saying:

"My serious Robert probably knows more about playing than I think. Will an affectionate goodnight suffice?"

He took her face between his hands then and studied it seriously for a moment, then kissed her lips gently.

"I've never seen you really happy before. Don't let your stepfather, or anybody else, quench it."

The light was still on in her stepfather's study. She knocked and put her head round the door to say goodnight. He was in the middle of a report, and merely echoed her goodnight.

In bed, her thoughts ranged over the evening. Perhaps, she thought, it was because the sight of Felix that evening had not evoked the usual mangled feelings of pain that her spirits had soared. It was as though she had seen the prison door of her unhappiness opening, had glimpsed another world beyond. Since Felix had told her the news on the bleak day in January, she had been living in a cell of desolation. But outside, she was discovering, the sun still shone, there was still kindness and companionship to be found.

Her affection for Felix never wavered, but the party that evening stayed in her mind always as a landmark; the evening when the pain he had inflicted slid away, when her heart came free of the past, when she felt on the threshold of a new life.

10

MORNING AND EVENING SONG

BRIDGET spent much of her free time during the next few weeks with Christine, finding her a happy, stimulating companion. Both of them lovers of the country, they walked for miles, Bridget still tracking down any points of interest for her history of the locality, and Christine enlightening her on the botanical side. Boris accompanied them on their expeditions, but their intention to use their walks as opportunities for training him was apt to get lost in their interest in their own conversation and their surroundings, and Boris followed his nose with zest and freedom. However, he was by instinct and the training of his forebears an obedient animal, and, when they remembered to instruct him, he fell in with their commands and added much to their enjoyment.

Christine was due to start a holiday with a field study group on Lundy at the beginning of September, before returning to the university. On their last afternoon together, they walked to Juniper Hill, a mile or two beyond Oakdene. The day was fine and warm, and Bridget took off her cardigan as they started to climb the sandy path up the hill. The flowers on the gorse bushes filled the air with their heavy fragrance. Already the berries on the mountain ash trees were a rich orange colour, and the brambles were red and purple. Boris stopped to chase a bee off a clump of heather, then ploughed on ahead of them, nose down, alert to any new scent. The path led them through a clump of pines to the top of the hill, with the whole expanse of the Weald before them and the smooth, rounded curves of the South Downs against the horizon. They found a gentle slope of heather and grass on which they could lie and look at the view.

"This holiday has been one of the nicest I can remember," said Christine, propped on one elbow, chewing a piece of grass, while Boris panted beside her.

"For me, too. Have an apple," said Bridget, fishing two rosy Worcesters out of her shoulder-bag.

"It's odd that you should have lived so near

us for so long, and we've only just got to know each other."

"M'm. I'm going to miss you now. It'll be fun on Lundy for you, though."

"Yes. They're not a bad gang, either. Be hard work, though. I haven't done as much as I should this vac. Not paper-work, that is. Weather's been too fine. Can't waste the sun. We don't get enough of it."

Below them, they could see the lanes threading their way round copses and fields like silver ribbons in the sun. Hedgerows formed a crazy pattern, and the grazing cattle looked like toys. In the mellow sunshine of early autumn, it was infinitely peaceful. On the main roads, traffic would be streaming along, but only the little lanes of England were visible from their look-out, and they were undisturbed. This is the England I love, thought Bridget; the forgotten lanes and drowsy fields, the little humped bridges and quiet streams, the woods and hills unchanged for centuries. And she prayed that she would never see them change.

Boris demolished their apple cores and stretched out again, head on paws, watching a red admiral butterfly sunning itself on a stone, too tired to investigate more closely.

"I suppose you couldn't come back with me this evening, Bridget?" asked Christine presently.

"I'd love to, but Father's due back from Germany tonight, and I must be home to get him a meal. He'll have had a hectic week in Europe. And didn't you say you'd be busy packing?"

"Yes. I wanted you as a buffer between me and Robert, though, because we had a skirmish this morning and I intend to go off to Lundy tomorrow without climbing down. It would be easier if a third party was present to keep us away from the field of conflict."

"Sorry. What was the skirmish about?"

"Oh, just a question of my independence of action," said Christine airily. "Time Robert realised that I'm grown up."

"Well, play it cool," said Bridget, smiling. "I speak as one very seldom able to play it cool, and so at a disadvantage."

"Me, too. And Robert plays it as cool as a cucumber, of course. That awful rationality of the legal mind! It's almost impossible to win. Just a case of holding out until I go tomorrow."

"You two get on very well as a rule, don't you?"

152

"Yes. But there comes a time when my dear brother's judicial rule must be challenged. He's horribly clever, though. Just when he's got you cornered with sound arguments which are irrefutable and you tell yourself that as a matter of principle you won't give in to such an inhuman machine, he brings out a sly bit of humour to rock you on your perch, and laughter's no help when you need a strong arm to bring down on his head. You just finish by tumbling down. This time, though, I'm staying remote and immovable."

"Well, good luck, but I won't stake any money on you. Robert's a tough proposition."

"M'm. He's ten years older than me, too. I wouldn't change him, but he's just got to learn one or two things. He's developed the dominating side of him a bit too much since our parents were killed. Only natural, I suppose. He had to pick up the pieces and carry on, and he's been very good to me. It changed him, you know. The accident. He used to be a great tease. Very lively. And with a widely ranging taste in girls."

"I'd never have guessed. Tell me more."

"Well, he liked them good-looking, but

that's about the only thing they had in common. There was a dark, haunting beauty who was an actress, a willowy creature with honey-coloured hair coiled in a bun who looked like a Sylphide but was a model, and an intense girl with great dark eyes and a lovely husky voice who was devoted to Oxfam and the underdeveloped countries and simply oozing social conscience. Then there was the athletic one who was terribly good at sailing and really looked zingy in stretch slacks and sweaters. I rather liked her. And there was one terrible female, all fair and fluffy, who kept looking at Robert with helpless big blue eyes. Robert's kitten, we called her. He had a bit of a job living her down."

"Who would have thought Robert a gay rover?" said Bridget, laughing.

"His girl friends only swam across our horizon briefly. He seldom brought them home. All this was years ago when I was a kid. He seemed to grow out of such pastimes and, as far as I know, hasn't looked at a girl for the past four or five years. Been too busy, perhaps. I always got on well with Robert, but I think I like the more sober version of the last two years best. He's taken on more authority, which has its trying aspects, of course, but he's kinder now than when he was younger, and we've grown closer. I've just got to make him realise that I'm twenty and not ten," concluded Christine cheerfully, recalling the stand to which she was committed.

Bridget smiled but said nothing. Christine might be twenty, but just then, in her crumpled cotton dress, with her hair escaping from its Alice band to hang round her face as she stooped to watch the progress of a beetle, she looked a child still. She wouldn't stand an earthly against Robert.

On Saturday evening, Robert called to return five shillings which Christine had borrowed from Bridget.

"She remembered it just as she was getting in the train, and asked me to repay it. Said she was sorry she'd forgotten all about it."

"So had I."

"She's a careless monkey."

"It didn't matter. Did you part on cordial terms?"

"Yes. Why? Oh, she told you about our small difference, did she?"

"No details. Just intimated that a stand was

being taken against certain encroachments on her independence."

"That was settled without much trouble," said Robert with a wry smile.

"I'm sure it was. I'm just going to make some coffee. You'll stay and have a cup, won't you?"

"Thanks. I'd like to. You're looking very well. Kit's enjoyed your company this holiday."

"The enjoyment was mutual. I like her. She's had a tonic effect. Wise Robert. Just what I needed," she said, teasing him.

"I'll send in my bill next week. How's work?"

"Flourishing. I had a letter from a publisher this morning. He'd read my articles in The Monitor and wants to know if I'd like to ferret out the local history of the whole county to make up a contribution to a book they are planning to publish in their County Series. They've already commissioned someone to deal with the flora and fauna, and other aspects will be covered by various contributors. Isn't it exciting?"

"Very. Who is the publisher?"

"Corrie and Birch."

"Oh yes. Adam Birch lives in these parts.

At Lynwood, I believe. A good opportunity for you, Bridget. Congratulations."

"Thank you. I shall love doing it, though I'll have to travel around a lot. The work I've already done only covers my own beat, which is a small part of the county."

He followed her into the kitchen and they talked about the project while she made coffee.

"If you'll take the tray into the sitting-room, Robert, I'll just take Father a cup and tell him you're here. It's time he stopped working. He's been at it all day."

Robert was studying the portrait of Bridget's mother when he heard Bridget calling him in a frightened voice. She was at the door of her stepfather's study, her face ashen.

"Robert. Father . . . I think he's had a stroke."

Owen Rainwood was slumped across his desk, the visible side of his face puckered up, one arm dangling over the side of his chair, breathing noisily. Robert loosened his collar and said quickly:

"Get the doctor, Bridget. Tell him he's had a stroke. Sling over a cushion, will you? Better not move him until the doctor gets here. Just keep him warm."

"Right. I'll get a hot water bottle and blankets."

She flew to the telephone, scarcely able to realise what had happened. When she returned to the study with blankets, Robert put an arm round her shoulders.

"This has been a shock. Go and heat up that coffee. There's nothing we can do."

And there was nothing that anybody could do. Her stepfather was removed to Ellarton hospital but did not regain consciousness. Bridget, Robert and his grandparents stayed at the hospital all night, but Owen Rainwood died in the early hours of the morning without any word for his family.

Mirabel asked to be left alone with her son for a few minutes before they left. When she rejoined them, her face austere and white, she said quietly:

"You must come back with us, Bridget dear. Robert will drive you home to fetch any things you need."

Back in the empty house, Robert waited while Bridget packed a small suitcase. When she rejoined him, he had made a pot of tea. It was nearly half past six and the sun was just rising on a dew-drenched morning.

"I wish," Bridget said, as they sipped their

tea, "I'd understood him better. Now it's too late. I never shall."

"He was a man very shut in on himself. I doubt whether anybody really knew him."

"He worked himself to death. I tried to tell him to ease up, but he never invited comment from me, and froze me if I tried to get close. It leaves an awful sense of failure. I think that's what Grandma was feeling at the hospital. When personal relationships that should be close fail, you can't help feeling that somehow you've been inadequate. He just didn't seem to care about anybody or anything except his work, after my mother died. And he wasn't even happy with her. I suppose work was his consolation."

"Yes. I think he knew this might happen. He made his will a few months ago, you know. I have a hunch that he'd been warned."

"Then why didn't he ease up?"

"Preferred to die in harness. Can you imagine him without his work?"

"No. He had nothing else. And his work was valuable to the country. After all, he was decorated for it."

"Yes. Well, come along, my dear. You look all in. We'll have to sort things out here some time, but just now it's bed and a sedative you want."

"I'm all right. I must see what I can do for Grandma and Grandpa."

"Yes. The old lady looked stricken. The second of her sons to go. But she's made of stern stuff. You'll be the one to be taken in hand. But they'll be glad to have you there."

And so they left the empty house behind them and drove through the quiet lanes to Melbridge. A new day was just beginning. The milkman was on his rounds. An early riser was exercising his dog on the Oakdene cricket field. Cobwebs sparkling with dew decorated the hedgerows, and the first yellowing of autumn could be seen on the lime trees by Melbridge church. Their message of the passing of time, of the mortality of all things, had never struck Bridget so poignantly before. "For though the day be never so long, at last the bells ringeth to evensong."

11

AUTUMN

ROBERT'S hunch that Owen Rainwood had known that his days were numbered was confirmed when he and Bridget began to go through the contents of his desk. In the top drawer was a sealed letter with Robert's name on it, and the words "To be opened after my death". Robert read the letter and handed it to Bridget.

Dear Robert,

I have reason to believe that my exit will not be long delayed, and that it may be sudden.

You, as my executor, will find all that you require in this desk or lodged with my Bank. Everything is in order. I wish you to destroy any personal papers I have left with the exception of the package tied with green tape at the back of the bottom drawer. This my wife left in my care to be given to Bridget when it seemed opportune. You will please give it to her.

My thanks for your good services.
Owen Rainwood

Bridget took the package off to her own
study, leaving Robert to his task. She
switched on the electric fire, for it was a chilly
day, and pulled up the rocking-chair, warm-
ing her hands before she opened the package.
Inside, she found some letters from her father
to her mother, written when he was in the
army. They were cheerful, affectionate, and
in all of them he mentioned the baby
daughter he had seen only once when on
leave from the Middle East. He had come
back to England in 1943, when there was a
gap in the letters. Bridget remembered her
mother telling her of the cottage in Devon
where they had lived for a year to be near her
father while he was stationed in England.
There was one more letter written just before
he went overseas in the first wave of the invasion of Europe. It was evident from all his
letters that his love for his wife and his
daughter was the core of his life. Then there
was a letter of sympathy and appreciation
from a fellow officer who had been with him
when he was killed, and a faded snapshot of

her father in the uniform of a Captain holding a baby in his arms. Bridget viewed with incredulous eyes the odd little scrap with the gummy smile and wispy hair that was Bridget Armadale. A small knitted boot-tee was between the snapshot and the friend's letter. Her father had apparently carried it round with him, for luck perhaps. A luck which had failed him. Then she saw a letter on the rug which she must have dropped. Picking it up, she recognised her stepfather's small, fine writing.

There was no date on it.

My dear Lorna,
You are right. We can't go on like this. Your face when I saw you off at the station a week ago has been haunting me ever since. We can neither of us stand any more bitter quarrels like the last.

I have been tortured all the week by the necessity to face the truth: that you do not and cannot love me; that try as you may, and I believe you when you say you have tried, you find it impossible to endure my love for you. I won't go into the old, old story of why you married me, knowing how you felt and how I felt; or whether I was to blame for persisting and wearing you down. Heaven knows we've talked enough on those lines. Now it is time to face the facts as they are and see what we can do with our wretched, battered marriage. It never was a marriage for you, I fancy. You married Paul, and are still married to Paul. He lives in your mind and your heart. He is the fourth person in my house. You, Paul and Paul's child all lined up against me. Paul eats at my table, lives in our bed. He was my friend. I hate him now as I have never hated anyone in my life before. Enough of that.

I love you too well. That is my pain. When I take you in my arms, you make me feel as though I am committing a criminal assault. You can bear it no longer, and nor can I. When you return with the child, it shall be as my wife in name only. You have my word for that. You say that you will not stand in the way of a divorce or a separation, but I see no reason for that. I shall never love another woman as I love you, and you are wedded to Paul until death. It sounds melodramatic, but it is a plain statement of fact that few people would believe. You have the gift of constancy to an inhuman degree, my dear. That being so, I would prefer you to continue to look after my home, and I will continue to be responsible for your welfare and your child's. That would at last spare me the humiliation of having the world know of my failure, and both of us the distress of making public our most private affairs. I can trust you to make a good showing as my wife, and it will be better for the child to have a secure and comfortable home, always your first concern, I know.

If you will let me know which train you will be on, I will meet you at Paddington. Have no fear. There will be no more recriminations, pleadings or demands. You have won. Or should I say Paul has won? I only know that it would have been better for me if I had never known either of you. We must try to retain some dignity in our lives, however. That is all that is left to us. Perhaps not all. I have my work. You have Paul's child.

That shall be the last word on it.

Yours,
Owen

So that was the explanation for her step-father's hostility, thought Bridget, distressed by the deep unhappiness which came through his deliberate, almost formal phrases. The letter of a man who did not find it easy to write of his emotions, and which seemed all the more bitter after the happy spontaneity of the letters which her father had written to his wife. She sat there, her mind back in the unhappy tangle of the past, until Robert came in.

"I've finished," he announced. "You look pale. Anything wrong?"

"No. I've been living with ghosts. Letters from my father to my mother when he was away in the army. And a letter from my stepfather to Mother, which explains a lot. I think you'd better read it."

He took the letter and after he had read it, he went to the window and stood staring out into the garden, as though pondering what he had read. Then he said quietly:

"Poor devil."

"Did you have any idea of this?" she asked.

"Roughly. Grandma talked about it to me one day. I hadn't realised things were so bad or that Uncle Owen had been so desperately involved. And you paid the price."

"We all paid the price. My mother, my stepfather and me. How different things would have been if my father had lived! I'm glad Mother left me his letters. I suppose she wanted me to know a little more about him, to know that they were happy and that I was part of their happiness. She never talked much of him. Perhaps it was too painful, or perhaps she was afraid of bringing his name up because of my stepfather."

"I wonder if she meant you to have this letter from Uncle Owen? I doubt it, somehow. It's harsh reading."

"I don't know. She could have forgotten it was there with the others. I feel very sorry for him now. I wish he could have forgotten the past and who I was."

"Well, it's over for you now, Bridget. You did all that you could, and a lot more than most girls would have done. Now you start a new chapter."

But the past was not over for either of them, and perhaps Bridget, at least, had some premonition of this, for she said slowly:

"These ghosts are not going to lie down quickly."

The whole Rainwood family attended the funeral at Melbridge church where Owen was buried close to his brother and his sister-in-law. He had left no instructions, so that his mother's wish that he should be brought to rest where other Rainwoods had come before him prevailed, although Arthur remarked wryly to his nephew Peter that it was the last resting-place old Owen would have chosen for himself, a remark which Peter considered in the worst of taste and ignored.

Afterwards, tongues wagged a little among the family when it was known that Owen had left only five hundred pounds to Bridget, and the remainder of his estate to medical research. It was a cardinal principle of the Rainwood family that money should be kept within the family, which was not wealthy.

"Don't know why they should be so shocked," said Arthur to Robert as they stood a little apart from the others that afternoon. "Owen had no time for the family, and Bridget wasn't his child, after all, though he might have been more generous to the girl. How she put up with him, I don't know. He gave me a chill every time I saw him."

Robert eyed his great-uncle with some amusement. There was something about his flamboyant full-bloodedness that defied all thoughts of mortality which such an occasion aroused. At seventy-three, his stocky figure and ruddy face reflected a vitality which his nephew Owen had never possessed. His abundant white hair sprang up from his head as though too lively for any anchorage, and the grey eyes under the bushy white eyebrows held a glitter in them which had little to do with age and which Mirabel maintained came from the devil. Fond of food, drink, good living, and still with an eye for pretty women, he was blessed with a vigorous good health that was a cause of affront to the more puritanical-minded members of the family and a sense of injustice in those who followed a more austere life and were rewarded with poorer health. If anybody should have a gastric ulcer or high blood pressure, they thought, it should be Arthur Rainwood, whose way of life asked for such inflictions, but he remained obstinately healthy and robust. Nevertheless, unless they were the particular victims of his tongue, they regarded this *enfant terrible* of the family with tolerance and some amusement. Victims, speechless with rage, had been known on their recovery to vow never to exchange another word with the old devil, but such vows were never kept unbroken for long since Arthur himself never took offence, only gave it, and breezily ignored hurt feelings.

"Bet Owen left more than might be expected," he went on. "Lived like a monk, after all, and was pretty highly paid for his valuable services, no doubt."

"No doubt," said Robert with a poker face. If Great-Uncle Arthur hoped to pump him, he was in for a disappointment.

"Well, I don't see any point in our wearing long faces. Owen's gone, God rest him, but it's hypocrisy to pretend that we shall miss him. Don't want anybody to be miserable at my funeral. Like everyone to have a jolly good party. Pretty hair that girl of Owen's got. Not red or gold. Don't see many like that. A nice mover, too," he added, his eyes watching Bridget cross the room with a plate of sandwiches. "What's she going to do now?"

"Live here for the time being. The grandparents are very fond of her, and Grandma thinks she needs a rest after the shock. The house and furniture will be sold as part of the estate."

"H'm. If you ask me, anything would be better than keeping house for Owen. However, *requiescat in pace* and all that. If I were her, I'd have a real fling with that modest legacy. I bet she's earned it. What wouldn't I give to be in my twenties again with a few hundred in my pocket and no ties! You young people don't know how to live. All so earnest and hard-working and committed. That girl looks as though she's got some spirit, and some good red blood in her. If I were younger, I'd enjoy showing her how to enjoy life, be gay. She'd respond, too, or I'm a Dutchman. No tame pigeon, that. Didn't I hear she'd taken a toss over Susan's husband?"

"I'm a bit remote from the family grape-vine," said Robert blandly.

"Plenty of fish in the sea. She doesn't want to pine over that one. Too young to tie herself down to a tame domestic life, anyway. Blest if I see why these young girls are so anxious to shut themselves up in a kitchen and spend their days washing nappies when the whole world's waiting to be enjoyed. I'm dry. Failing anything better, I shall have to get another cup of tea."

Robert watched him cross the room to Mirabel, who was dispensing tea with her customary dignity but looking desperately tired and worn. Was his great-uncle really so callous and blind to other people's sensibilities as he appeared, or was he afraid to treat life as anything but a toy balloon for his amusement? Or was he simply an egomaniac, determined to enjoy himself at all costs? Tiring suddenly of the chatter, Robert, who had seen Bridget slip out of the french door, followed her example and went in search of her. He found her at the end of the garden, watching a red admiral butterfly sunning itself on a clump of Michaelmas daisies.

"Hullo, there. Tired of the crowd?"

"A little. Not in the mood."

"Nor I. A good thing for the grandparents when this day is over. When are you going to fetch your personal belongings from the house?"

"Tomorrow. I've brought most of my clothes. It's only a question of my papers and typewriter and the few things in my study that were mine. And the portrait of my mother."

"There's no need to be so punctilious about leaving everything. His instructions were to sell up after you'd taken anything you particularly wanted."

"I know. But apart from the portrait of my mother, there's nothing more of his that I want."

"It hurt you that he left you so little?"

"Only because it exemplified his attitude to me. The money doesn't matter and it's gone to a good cause, but after all these years I'd have liked some message of goodwill, some indication that I was a little more than an unpleasant duty thrust on him."

"Now that you know the reason why, you don't need to take it so personally. You were a symbol to him, that's all. A scapegoat."

"Yes. It's peaceful here in the garden," she said, sitting on a wooden seat under the oldest and largest apple tree in the orchard.

"If one of those apples falls on your head, it'll brain you. I've never seen such whoppers."

"They won't fall. They're not ripe yet. What a sad little song the robin sings in the autumn. He's up there in the pear tree."

"You'll be happier, living here, Bridget."

"Yes. I haven't made up my mind whether to keep on as a freelance, or take a job and write in my spare time."

"What sort of a job?"

"Oh, on a magazine, perhaps, or a newspaper. But it would mean going to London, and that doesn't appeal to me very much. I must be independent, though, and I don't earn a lot with freelance work. In any case, I shall finish the work for the Corrie and Birch book first."

"Take it easy. You've earned a break. This last year has been a trying one for you. Shall I bring the car to fetch your chattels tomorrow?"

"Would you, Robert? That would help a lot. I was wondering whether to take Grandfather's truck and rouse everybody's interest by wheeling it from Rushleigh to Melbridge. Grandma's giving me the little gable room looking over the garden for my study."

"I've got to go in to the office tomorrow morning. A nuisance. I loathe going up on Saturdays, but this client couldn't come any other time. I could be round at the house about half past two tomorrow afternoon, though. Suit you?"

"Fine. You've been so good to me, Robert. I don't know what I should have done without your help."

"Well, Uncle Owen appointed me to be his executor."

"I wasn't meaning only that. I've a lot more to thank you for."

"I'll remind you next time you fly out at me," he said, with a little smile.

"Oh, it's always a very brief rebellion. Nothing you can't brush off."

"I wonder. I've a feeling that when you've breathed the heady air of freedom for a little and are happy again, you might be quite difficult to handle. Great-Uncle Arthur's a shrewd old bird, for all his capers."

"And what does Great-Uncle Arthur know about me?"

"He has an eye for certain points, based, no doubt, on his long experience with the ladies. Circumstances have all conspired to dim you this past year and make you comparatively docile."

"And shall we quarrel because I'm happy? That's an odd philosophy."

"We shall quarrel," he said imperturbably, "and make it up, I hope."

"We shall quarrel and I shall give in, you mean."

"Could be. Anyway, be happy. I'll take the consequences."

The sun was sinking and its slanting rays filtered through the orchard in a chequered pattern and bathed the back of the house in a mellow, golden light. The robin's plaintive little song suited the autumn mood. They fell silent, both reluctant to rejoin the family,

content to sit there in a quiet mood of reflection, drawing comfort from each other's
presence on a day whose chill message was
that all things pass.

12

BREDON LODGE

BRIDGET had never fully realised the blight which her stepfather had cast over her life until she experienced the different climate of life at Bredon Lodge. There, with warmth and affection and freedom always present as natural elements, she began to know a happiness she had never known before. Her stepfather's biting sarcasm and too-polite hostility had built up in her over the years a repression of all feelings which might offer a target and a sense of guilt which was like a hair shirt. Only when she was relieved of these pressures did she realise how cramped and strained her life had been, and she felt herself expanding as though she had emerged from a chrysalis and was only now learning the joy of freedom in the sunshine.

The change in her was too striking to go unremarked, even by one so unobservant as her grandfather, who said to his wife one morning after he had left Bridget working on his new rock garden:

"How that girl's blossomed out here, Mirabel! Happy as a lark. Used to be such a quiet, reserved girl. Always a bit on the defensive, I thought. I hardly recognise her."

"Yes. I watched Owen dampen her down over the years after Lorna died, but she kept the real core of herself intact, thank goodness! She has a rare gift for happiness. It's a joy to have her here."

"She's making a splendid job of that bed for the stream. Bless me, if I'm not careful, she'll take the whole project out of my hands!"

"Well, you're not either of you to lift heavy stones about. Leave that to Bryn," said Mirabel firmly.

"Yes, dear. She's got a good eye for landscape gardening. Really interested. Bubbling over. I do like people who are keen. Our grandchildren often seem to me so bored and indolent. Look at young Nick. Almost too much trouble for him to talk."

"We're getting old, Charles, and the gap is a big one to cross. He probably has plenty to say to his contemporaries."

"Take young Susan last weekend, then.

178

Looked as animated as a stuffed doll and hardly a word to say for herself."

"I think she and Felix had fallen out."

"What about?"

"Bills."

"She's an extravagant young woman, I expect. Couldn't expect anything else, the way her father's indulged her."

"She thinks Felix ought to take the job Peter has offered him and earn more money, and then there wouldn't be any trouble over bills. Her father refuses to help her now that she's married."

"Quite right, too. It's a husband's duty to support his wife. Surprised at Peter being firm for once."

"I think he's trying to force Felix's hand. In fact, I rather suspect that Susan and her father have agreed on the tactics."

"What makes you think that, my dear? I never get wind of any of these goings-on."

"Oh, I had a chat with Joyce last weekend, and she has an ingenuous way of revealing far more than she realises. Peter should leave the young people to manage their own affairs and not conspire with Susan to force Felix into a job he doesn't want."

"A wife should be loyal to her husband,"

said Charles gruffly. "Do Susan good to have to manage on a modest income for a change. Bridget thinks another dam across the stream lower down would be an improvement. Came in to get the plan."

Mirabel smiled as she watched him trudge down the garden, plan in hand, to join Bridget. They stood looking at the plan, absorbed, the tall, thin man in corduroy trousers and an old tweed coat patched at the elbows, his carefully brushed, sparse grey hair revealing a bald patch in the middle, and the slender figure of the girl beside him in dark green slacks and sweater, her hair standing out bright in the greyness of the November morning. What a lot Owen had deprived himself of, she thought. How foolish to let disappointment and jealousy live on to warp your life and spread its cruelty like a cancer. In rejecting Bridget, he had impoverished his life still further.

For Bridget, absorbed in her work for the Corrie and Birch book, autumn slid into winter all too quickly. The assignment was a full-time one, for it entailed a lot of travelling for research in the less familiar parts of the county, and she had promised her contribution by the end of the year. She was discussing it with Robert one Saturday afternoon in early December as they walked across the heath with Boris.

"I had the photographer with me on Monday. We're using half a dozen photographs. It was a fine day and we enjoyed ourselves."

"When will the book be published?"

"Mr. Birch said they aim to publish next September. The other contributors include some well-known names, so I feel proud to be in their company. It's been an absorbing job and I've enjoyed it more than anything I've ever done before. I got in a bit of a panic a few weeks ago when I thought I wouldn't get it finished anywhere near the time I'd promised, but I put a spurt on and I think I'll just make it before Christmas."

Boris came lolloping up with a stick in his mouth and Robert obligingly threw it.

"Any plans after that?"

"No. My mind's been too occupied to give it much thought, and I haven't decided yet what kind of a job I want, but I must tackle it after Christmas."

"You're very happy with the grandparents, aren't you?"

"Yes. I don't think I've ever been so happy as

I've been in the last months. It's been marvellous not to need any defences. And although in many ways, Grandma and Grandpa are very old-fashioned, and Grandma can be a martinet, they're amazingly kind and tolerant, and not in the least constricting. It's taken for granted, of course, that one conforms to a certain standard of conduct," concluded Bridget, smiling.

"I'm glad it's turned out so well. A transformation in you. Less than a year ago, I thought you were the most bedraggled, unhappy young creature I'd ever seen."

"It seems awfully remote, that old life."

"All of it?" asked Robert, looking at her searchingly.

"All of it."

"Good. I'm glad your stepfather proved wrong. He said that you'd spend the rest of your life looking back at the sun that was Felix."

"It was my stepfather who lived in the past."

"Yes. I've often thought of that letter. Few men could have been so tortured and unhappy."

They had come to the pond and Bridget remained silent as they stood there watching the ripples swept by the wind across the surface of the water in swift dark shadows. It had been a grey day, but the sun had emerged from beneath a bank of cloud as it was setting, and now the sky was streaked with red in the west. The pond was fringed with fine silver sand, in a landscape of silver birches, bracken and heather that had a strange melancholy beauty on that wintry afternoon. Boris had a drink there, but did not venture in.

In a sudden access of energy, she picked up a stick and ran along the edge of the pond brandishing it in front of Boris, who pranced delightedly after her, trying to reach the stick. They had a tug of war, Boris getting a firm foothold in the sand, Bridget laughing as he tugged this way and that. Robert, watching them, thought how attractive this new re-vitalised Bridget was. In a suède jacket that matched the dead bracken, mustard-coloured tweed skirt, and a bright green silk scarf tucked in at the neck of her jacket, her hair blowing away from her laughing face, she brought warmth and life to the darkening landscape. Less submissive and ready to be led by him than she had been when un-happiness had sapped her will, he found her now a heart-warming, stimulating companion, and if her resilience made her a very lively ball to handle, the challenge found him ready. The tussle between Bridget and Boris ended in a draw, for the stick broke and Boris went off proudly with his half, and Bridget rejoined Robert, saying:

"Kit will see a difference in Boris when she comes home. He's too strong for me now. I had a letter from her yesterday. She says you're a bad correspondent and what are you up to not to be able to spare her more than half a page at a time?"

"That says all that's necessary. Kit's pen is as free as her tongue, as you've no doubt discovered."

"She's a racy correspondent."

"I suppose you two will be jaunting off together during the vacation."

"Yes. I hope you'll join us when you can."

"Perhaps."

"That sounds a bit unenthusiastic."

"Two's company."

"I'll remember to leave Kit for you at the weekends," said Bridget gravely.

"That's not what I meant, and you know it."

"What a delicate situation for two females who are pining for your lordship's company.

What shall we do? Try to ditch each other? But neither of us would want to do that," said Bridget, her eyes dancing as she looked up at him.

"You don't look as though you're pining for anything or anybody just now."

"I'm not. It's good to be heartfree. I feel like an escaped balloon."

"Determined never to be tethered again?"

"Not yet, anyway."

"Very sensible of you."

"I'm glad we have the same outlook," said Bridget demurely.

Robert's lips twitched as he looked down at a pair of innocent grey eyes, and he ruffled her hair with a friendly hand as he replied:

"So am I."

Something in his expression brought a flush to her cheeks, and she said hurriedly:

"If we're not to be late for Grandma's Saturday tea, we'd better be moving."

It was nearly dark by the time they reached the car, which Robert had parked at the edge of the heath. With Boris stowed away in the back, they drove to Melbridge. From the cars in the drive at Bredon Lodge, it seemed as though there would be a pretty full muster of the Rainwood family at this Saturday tea.

Mirabel had established the custom of a family gathering for tea at Bredon Lodge on the first Saturday of every month as soon as the first of her six children had married, and she expected a good reason for any absentees, of whatever generation. It had worked well as a means of keeping the family together, and since the tea hour was all that Mirabel insisted on, the commitment did not weigh heavily on the young people who might have other ways of wishing to spend the evening.

Bridget, hungry after her walk, eyed with pleasure the long table with its immaculate damask cloth and pretty china, as she sat down between Great-Aunt Lucille and Robert. There were plates of brown and white bread and butter, scones, cucumber sandwiches and cress sandwiches, dishes of home-made blackcurrant jam, a large fruit cake, plates of congress tarts, jam tarts and rock cakes, and a sponge sandwich.

"I haven't sat down to an English tea for years," said Lucille in her pretty, lilting voice. "I didn't realise that Mirabel still kept her Saturday teas going. All these carbohydrates!"

"They won't bite you," said Robert, grinning.

"All I ever have is a cup of China tea with a slice of lemon and nothing to eat. And Mirabel still has the family tea service. I always did like it. How she's kept it intact through all these years, I can't imagine. It belonged to our mother, you know," added Lucille, picking up the white china plate with the border of pink roses and tapping it appreciatively. "And do you know, I saw the identical service last time I was in Nassau."

Lucille paid a regular winter visit to Nassau and she needed little prodding from Bridget now to tell them more about it.

"I'm going with business in mind this January, though," she concluded. "I plan to open a salon in Nassau. Great scope there, I think. I may need your professional advice, Robert."

"Always at your service, Aunt Lucille."

"You may not be so cautious as your father always was over my business deals. At heart, I don't think he ever accepted that women ought to be in control of any business, and he looked on all my schemes for expansion as risky. He thought I'd be the prey of all the male wolves in business, and saw that my contracts were always more than water-tight."

"I think he did realise in the end that you could make rings round them all," said Robert.

"If he did, he thought it quite unnatural. And you're writing a book, dear, I hear," said Lucille to Bridget.

"Not a book. Contributing to one. My part only amounts to about a fifth," said Bridget, offering Lucille a plate of jam tarts, which she refused as though offered a fatal dose of poison.

"How splendid to be able to sample all these delicious things and keep the figure of a sylph," said Lucille admiringly as Bridget embarked on her second jam tart.

There were fourteen of them present that day and the chatter was continuous. Bridget, absent from these gatherings while her stepfather was alive, had come to enjoy them since living at Bredon Lodge. The Rainwoods got on pretty well together, for all the criticism which went on between the various branches, so that the tea-parties were good-humoured affairs and the three generations seemed to blend harmoniously enough during the short time they were brought together.

Felix and Susan left first, as they were

going to a dance in Ellarton that evening. It was part of Bridget's new-found freedom that she could now meet Felix without any sense of strain, and she realised how much her dependence on him in the past had been caused by her isolation from all warmth and friendliness. While Susan went upstairs with her grandmother to fetch her coat, Felix sought out Bridget in a corner of the drawing-room.

"I haven't had a word with you for ages, Biddy. You're not deliberately avoiding me, are you?"

"Of course not, Felix," she said, smiling. "How are things with The Monitor?"

"All right. I just need more hours in the days. I miss you."

"No assistant editor?"

"I've decided to do without and manage myself. Your work going well?"

"Yes. I've almost finished."

"So you've got between the hard covers of a book before me, after all," he said with an odd little smile.

"What about that novel of yours?"

"No time for that now. I guess it wasn't very good, anyway."

He looked thin and tired, and there was

something in the way he was looking at her that made her uneasy.

"How well you're looking these days, Biddy," he went on as she said nothing.

"It must be the carefree life I have now," she said lightly.

"Oh, come, things weren't so bad before, were they? We've had good times together."

"I wouldn't go back for the world," she said quietly.

"I would."

"Don't say that, Felix," she said, wishing that Robert would stop looking at her from the other side of the room and come to her rescue.

"I can't help it. It's the truth. Marriage imposes a lot of chains I hadn't expected."

"You'd better cheer up or Susan's going to find you a grim partner at the dance. And here she is."

To Bridget's disappointment, Robert left soon after, pleading work.

"Working at the weekend. That's bad," she said, shaking her head. "What about that course of frivolity we prescribed for each other last summer? When are you going to have time for that?"

"I rather thought you were engaged on some urgent work, too."

"Not at weekends. We all need to let up sometimes."

"Agreed. I call walking over the heath with you and Boris letting up. I don't think I'm a good candidate for more frivolous pastimes."

"You knew how to be frivolous once," she said, teasing him.

"Tell me more."

"Not for me to go into details, but I gathered from Kit that in your early twenties you were a very gay spark with a wide range of frivolous activities."

She had walked out with him to the car, and standing beside him on that dark, wintry evening, she felt the force of his personality, the pulling power which seemed to strengthen with every meeting, in spite of some instinct of resistance which she could hardly explain. Perhaps it was her own will resisting too dominant a person, or perhaps it was a caution in her based on her painful experience with Felix. She had been quite honest when she had told him that she wished to stay heartfree. The old scars had only recently healed, and she wanted to keep away from fire now. But Robert was beginning to present a challenge to her which was hard to resist. He was too serious-minded. At thirty, work and responsibilities governed his life. She wanted to lighten the pattern, see if anything remained of the young Robert.

"Kit has a habit of making everything highly-coloured," he said non-committally.

"Life is real, life is earnest. And you're not going to let me tempt you to have fun, then."

"You might get more than you bargained for."

"I'll chance it."

"You haven't got red hair for nothing. I'll bear your advice in mind. But I'm still working this evening, so stop offering me blandishments and run along in before you catch cold."

"Prosaic to the end," she said in mock despair. "Back to the legal documents. Cakes and ale are not for you. I shall call you Malvolio."

"Why are you complaining? You've young Nick and Rupert in there to work on. Why waste your efforts on such unpromising material?"

"It's the reforming zeal in me."

"I stopped letting young women educate me years ago, my dear."

"I'm utterly crushed. I'll say no more."

"Good." He got into the car, then wound down the window and added: "By the way, I've a couple of tickets for the concert in Ellarton next Saturday evening. Brahms and Beethoven. Care to come?"

"Love to."

"Right. I'll be round for you about six-thirty, then. So long."

"Clever Robert," she said, laughing. "Always the last word."

He waved his hand, gave a stern command to Boris, who had woken from his sleep and was cavorting about on the back seat signalling his pleasure at seeing Robert, and moved off down the drive, leaving Bridget smiling ruefully after him.

13

A PRESENT

THE misgivings which Bridget had felt over that short exchange with Felix at the Saturday tea-party were not allayed when she met him unexpectedly in a café in Ellarton two weeks later. She had been buying Christmas presents and had gone into the café for a mid-morning coffee, laden with parcels. Tucking herself away at a corner table for two, her parcels piled on the vacant chair, she had just ordered her coffee when Felix came in. She saw his tall figure hovering by the door as he looked round, and she hastily picked up the menu and dropped her head to study it. In a moment, his voice said:

"Hullo, Biddy. Can I join you?"

He swept her parcels from the chair and put them down in the corner behind her, saying:

"Looks as though you've had a good haul."

"Yes. I've completed my list now. Have you forsaken your usual dive for coffee?"

"Yes. They've installed taped music which I loathe. Don't usually bother about coffee these days, but I make an exception on Saturday mornings. All geared up for the Rainwood Christmas party?"

"Yes. I'm looking forward to it."

"We're going away. I expect you've heard."

"Yes. Grandma doesn't really approve, but Uncle Peter insisted that Aunt Joyce needed a rest and that you and Susan were keen on the idea."

"Sue is. And I shall prefer the Torquay hotel to spending Christmas at my in-laws' house, which was the alternative. There'll be some dancing at the hotel and a floor show. And my father-in-law insists on footing the bill," he concluded dryly.

"Should be fun."

"M'm. That's a pretty dress. What colour would you call it?"

"The girl who sold it to me called it blue grotto, if that helps."

"It doesn't. Nearer to a blue cedar. Anyway, it suits you. You're very easy on the eye these days, Biddy. Who'd have expected it from that freckly little tadpole with the carroty hair?"

The waitress arrived just then with their coffee and Bridget made no reply. Felix stirred his coffee reflectively for a few moments, then said jerkily:

"You and Robert Rainwood, Biddy. You're around together a bit these days, I believe. Anything in it?"

"We're good friends."

"Nothing more?"

"Nothing more, but it isn't really your business, Felix, is it?" she said gently.

"Of course it is. We're old friends. You're not going back on that just because I'm married, are you?"

"It makes a difference. You must realise that. Especially in view of Susan's attitude. You can't have two lives, Felix. The new one you chose blots out the old one."

"I'll never accept that. We grew up together. I haven't found so many good friends that I can afford to jettison the best of the bunch. Marriage shouldn't be as claustrophobic as that."

"I think you're being unrealistic."

"I've never felt more realistic in my life," he said with an odd little smile. "When I came in just now and saw you there, it was as though the sun had come out, and I realised then just how much you'd contributed to my life in the past. Whether I'm married or not, you knitted yourself into my life in those years, Biddy, and you'll always be there."

"Whatever we contributed to each other's lives in the past, we can have nothing to do with each other's future. You chose to take a different path, and so have I, now. They can't come together again."

"Have you really chosen a different path now, Biddy?"

Her eyes met his steadily as she said:

"Yes, Felix. I've finished with the past. I'm happy in the present. There are no ghosts haunting me now. Only happy memories of a good friend which I wouldn't want spoilt."

"That's the truth?"

"That's the truth, Felix."

He looked down at his coffee and was silent. She could not tell what he was thinking, and glanced at her watch, seeking an excuse to escape now that there was no more to be said, but he saw her and said quickly:

"Spare me a little more time. It may be our last opportunity and there are things I want you to know."

"Isn't it pointless, saying any more?"

"Tell me, Biddy. If I'd asked you to marry

me, you would have said yes, wouldn't you?"

"I don't think you've the right to ask that now."

"You would have married me, wouldn't you?" he insisted.

"At the time, yes. But you were right about us when you said we were fond of each other, but we weren't in love with each other. There's a difference. At the time, your engagement to Susan knocked the bottom out of my world because your friendship was the only warm thing in it. Since my stepfather died and my life has broadened out, I've realised that what I lost when you married was good friendship, no more. And the gap has been filled now by new companions. That's not to say that I don't value what was. My life would have been unendurable without your companionship after my mother died. I shall always be grateful to you for that, Felix. But it's in the past. And must stay there."

"You say we weren't in love. That would have come. I could have . . ."

"Please, Felix. It's foolish and unfair to Susan and to me to start speculating. Our paths have gone off in different directions. You must accept that. You love Susan, don't you? I've never seen two people as much in love as you two were."

"Oh yes, I suppose so. But she's not like you, Biddy. She doesn't understand what my work means to me. She's not interested. Can't see why I won't accept her father's offer and be comfortably off for the rest of our lives. She should have married a rich man."

"I expect all married couples have difficulties of adjustment for the first year, and Susan's very young."

"And spoiled. Her father makes a fool of her. If it weren't for him, I might make her see my point of view. He dishes her up with the story that if I really cared for her, I'd want to earn more money and keep her in the style she's always been used to."

Bridget looked at his thin, sensitive face and could find nothing to say.

"It's not as if she makes the slightest effort to keep within our means," he went on. "I pinch and scrape on my side, but Sue hasn't a clue about managing or any desire to learn. Final demands and bills that have to be shuffled every month to keep the least urgent at the bottom of the pile are a bit dampening to that first fine careless rapture, I can tell you."

199

"I'm sorry I can't help you, Felix, and I feel I shouldn't be listening."

"I know. It's just that there's nobody I can talk to about it, and I was feeling a bit desperate this morning. And seeing you made the cork come out. You'd have worked your fingers to the bone to help me keep The Monitor going. It struck me then, what I'd thrown away. I wanted you to know. I won't ever mention it again. If I weren't a selfish devil, I'd say I'm glad that you're happy and free of the past. I'll say it, anyway, and try to mean it. But, Biddy, what I'd give to put the clock back!"

"This is just a bad patch. You're over-worked and worried. You'll come out of it and be happy again, I'm sure."

He walked to the bus stop with her and left her there. Watching his tall figure wend its way along the crowded pavement of the High Street, she felt helpless and troubled. He was devoted to his calling as a journalist and if Susan thought that unimportant when weighed against the large salary and good prospects he would have in her father's organisation, she did not know Felix. Her thoughts were interrupted by the horn of a car which had drawn up beside her.

"Hop in," said Robert. "I'll run you home."

Stowing herself and her parcels beside him on the front seat, she wondered if he had seen Felix. Past gossip, and loyalty to Felix who had spoken to her in confidence, made her reluctant to mention the encounter, and as Robert needed all his concentration to get through the tangle of traffic, she remained silent. It was not until they had emerged from the town and Robert took the fork which led to Oakdene and Melbridge, that the silence between them was broken by him.

"As Christmas gets closer and traffic worse, a misanthropic gloom seems to descend on me. It'll be impossible to get lunch anywhere in the City next week for Christmas celebrations. I usually send out for coffee and sandwiches in the run-up period to Christmas."

"Poor Robert. You do seem to be allergic to fun."

"Depends what you mean by fun. All this orgy of eating and drinking and shopping is not what I call fun."

"I enjoy it."

"So it seems," he said dryly, and she stole a quick glance at him, wondering whether there was more behind those few words than was obvious. His face revealed nothing more than a rather grim concentration on the road ahead, and she decided that he was out of sorts and definitely not in a mood to be told about her accidental meeting with Felix.

When he dropped her at Bredon Lodge, he refused to go in, saying briskly:

"I'm picking up Miss Mellon at Farrow's farm at half past twelve. She wanted a consultation with Farrow about the turkey. I shall have to step on it."

"Well, thank you for the lift, Robert. I wouldn't have been popular on the bus with all these parcels. There's nothing wrong, is there? Apart from the imminence of Christmas, I mean?"

"Isn't that enough?" he said, but he gave her the slow smile which these days seemed to have a very peculiar effect on her, and waved a friendly hand as he drove off.

She would have to analyse that peculiar effect one day, she thought, looking after the car. Meanwhile, she could count neither of her encounters that morning as exactly reassuring.

Her grandmother came out into the hall

with a letter in her hand as soon as Bridget closed the front door behind her.

"Hullo, dear. I've some interesting news here for you. A letter from Great-Aunt Lucille. She wants to know if you would like to go to the Bahamas with her in January."

Dumping her parcels on the chest in the hall, Bridget followed Mirabel into the drawing-room, a little breathless at this news.

"How kind of her! Tell me more."

"It's not quite as altruistic as it sounds," said Mirabel a little wryly. "My brother, James, has decided that he would like to get away from the English winter weather this year and go, too. Lucille has business matters to attend to over there, and it would suit her to have you with her to keep an eye on James, and also type any letters that might arise from her business negotiations. Neither of them arduous undertakings, and you would be free to enjoy yourself for much of the time. She aims to return early in March. Does it appeal to you?"

"Very much," said Bridget, who felt that quite apart from the pleasure of flying from January bleakness into sunshine, it would be a timely interval away from the complications of Felix, during which she could ponder on those peculiar sensations aroused lately by Robert, and decide, too, on the kind of job to look for on her return.

"You'll need some clothes. Lucille, as always, will be staying at the most expensive hotel," said Mirabel.

"I'll telephone her tonight. Is she in the London flat or in Sussex with Uncle James?"

"In London. I'm so glad Lucille thought of this. She said you seemed interested in the Bahamas last time she was here, and she's taken a fancy to you. Lucille always did have a shrewd eye for picking people who will be useful to her, and the skill to make it sound like pure goodness of heart and generosity of mind. However, whatever the motives, it will be a delightful experience for you, dear."

And with this, Bridget whole-heartedly agreed.

When she told Robert about it on Christmas Eve, he gave her a pensive stare and said:

"It will be good for you. Broaden your horizon and help you to get the past into the right perspective."

Which observation she found extremely irritating. Fortunately Kit, perched on a ladder tying mistletoe over the door, was so excited by the news that she poured out a string of questions which enabled Bridget to ignore Robert's remark.

"Don't know why you're putting all these decorations up here, Kit," he said when asked later to hold the end of a paper garland while Kit went up the ladder again. "We're spending Christmas Day and Boxing Day at Grandma's, and there won't be any parties here."

"I like it to look festive. Don't be such an old Scrooge."

"I'm merely being rational. Who do you expect to linger under the mistletoe, for example?"

"You never know. Hand me up that other ball of thread, will you? Careful."

Bridget rescued the garland from Robert's indifferent hand just before it was stretched to breaking-point, and he left the two girls to it.

"Don't know what's bitten him," said Kit cheerfully. "He's been very gritty this week. I suggested that his liver was affected by drinking too much at office celebrations, perhaps, but that didn't seem to go down very well. By the way, Felix Parvey offered me a lift home from the station this evening, and gave me a package for you. Said he was on his way to deliver it, but when I told him you were coming here tonight he left it with me to give you. Something about the typescript of some old articles of yours that you wanted. Now where did I put it?"

A search for the package among the clutter of paper decorations, holly, mistletoe, string, twine, scissors and wrapping-paper proved fruitless. Bridget was mystified. She had not asked Felix for any typescript.

"Robert," bawled Kit from the doorway, "do you know what I did with that parcel Felix Parvey left with me for Bridget?"

"I'm not deaf," observed Robert from the hall. "You dumped it in my study with the present you'd got for Mellie. And I don't want paper chains in my study."

"Oh yes, I remember. I put it there for safety. Robert, those aren't the paper chains I put up with such artistic care in your study, are they?"

"Yes. They brushed my head every time I walked under them, and made my study look like a bazaar. Here, take 'em. I'll get Bridget's parcel."

Unceremoniously thrusting the pile of paper chains into Kit's hands, he ignored her complaints and went back to his study. He brought the parcel into the sitting-room and handed it ceremoniously to Bridget.

"Take it and put it with your things. It's liable to get lost in this shambles and I wouldn't want important papers to go astray," he said with a sardonic lift to his eyebrows which made her want to hit him. That the package was far too hard to contain papers was as obvious to her as to him.

"Thanks," she said, and took it out to the hall.

She was aware of a new, dangerous Robert that evening. He joined them for coffee and it seemed to her that all his remarks were barbed, that the dark blue eyes, usually so friendly, now watched her with an anger that was more disturbing because it was under such cold control. Kit seemed unaware of these undercurrents, and chattered away happily. Robert lit his pipe, and bided his time. Then, while Kit took the coffee tray out, he fired his first shot, saying smoothly:

"By the way, would those papers include the article you did on the local history of Oakdene? I never did manage to get hold of that."

"I don't think so," said Bridget, and then could have bitten off her tongue.

"Don't think so?" pounced Robert. "But you must know what you asked for."

"I didn't ask for that article."

"Pity. What did you ask for? There might be some more I missed."

"I suggest you wait until the book's published," she said sweetly, her anger now aroused by his inquisition.

"That package contains no papers, and you know it."

"I don't think it's any business of yours, Robert."

"No? Just put it down to idle curiosity. A loving gift from your old friend, perhaps?"

"I've no idea."

"You could open it, or is it likely to contain a message too intimate to share?"

"I find you too objectionable to talk to any more."

"And I find it objectionable to have my sister used as a go-between for you and Parvey."

"How dare you say that?"

"How simple do you think I am?"

"I don't think you're simple. No mind as unpleasant and suspicious as yours is simple."

"What you and Parvey do may be your

business now, but unless you're very careful, it'll blow up into being the business of a good many members of the family, and a very unsavoury business it will be. However, I'm past the stage of trying to protect you from your own folly. Just don't try to invite me to share in your fun, too. Confine the fun to one male at a time, will you? Or I might get rather annoyed."

"Oh, your high-and-mighty attitude is insufferable. Just because I receive a package from Felix, I'm supposed to be carrying on an affair with him. Surely your professional training should demand more evidence than that."

"Not just a package. All the past, my dear. Your stepfather said you'd never give it up, and I guess you won't. Secret meetings, presents. Where do you think it's going to end?"

Kit came back and even she could not fail to see that Bridget's flushed cheeks and sparkling eyes and Robert's cold scrutiny did not add up to casual *bonhomie*.

"Are you two quarrelling?" she asked with her usual frankness.

"Certainly not," said Robert calmly. "Just

trying to reconcile two different points of view on what constitutes fun."

"Don't let his Scrooge-like attitude to Christmas goad you into trying to convert him, Bridget. He's set in his ways."

"He certainly is. I must be going, Kit, or I'll miss the last bus."

"Robert will run you home, won't you, Robert?"

"Delighted."

"I think I shall find the bus more fun," said Bridget cuttingly.

"Very likely. But you've missed it, I'm afraid. This clock's stopped, and I don't blame it after being shrouded in all that ivy. It's ten-thirty. The last bus for Melbridge left five minutes ago, so I'm afraid you'll have to accept the duller alternative of my car."

There was nothing else for it. She would have walked if it had been at all possible, but ten miles at that time of night could not be tackled even in the wild state of anger in which she found herself.

In the car, she said coldly:

"I met Felix quite unexpectedly in Latimer's on Saturday morning when I was having coffee there. That is what you mean by 'secret meetings', I suppose."

"You didn't mention it when I drove you home."

"I don't have to tell you everything that happens to me. And you didn't seem in a very sympathetic mood."

"You won't ever find me sympathetic about goings-on between you and Felix."

"Goings-on! You have absolutely no foundation for saying that. I haven't been alone with Felix since I left The Monitor last summer until we bumped into each other on Saturday. I told you. That's over. For some unaccountable reason, you seem unable to believe it."

"Let's draw up here and have it out. I don't like arguing and driving."

He parked the car on a grassy clearing beside the lane and slid one arm along the back of her seat as he turned to her.

"I saw, as perhaps nobody else did, what it meant to you to lose Felix. Your stepfather was convinced that you would always love him."

"Because he interpreted everything in the light of the past. His past. The cases are quite different. My mother had been married to the man she loved for years, had borne his child. There's no comparison between that and my friendship with Felix. You're obsessed with my stepfather's point of view. I wish I'd never shown you that letter now. It's made you quite unable to view my position rationally."

"If I'm anything, I'm a rational animal," replied Robert grimly. "I believed you when you said that the past was remote to you now, and no longer counted. Then I see you and Felix together, and discover that Kit, as green a girl as ever lived, bless her, is acting as a go-between because presumably Felix is afraid to deliver a present to Bredon Lodge where it would be noticed by the grandparents, perhaps. Knowing how jealous Susan is, and the talk about you and Felix that started before, why should you take the risk of arousing more trouble if Felix really means nothing to you now?"

"I didn't say 'nothing'. He was my friend. I shall always feel affectionately towards him, that's all. I know nothing about the parcel, and don't imagine it is a present. Probably something I left at the office. A dictionary, perhaps. I just don't know. And as the meeting with Kit was quite by chance, deep-laid schemes to by-pass the grandparents are obviously ridiculous and figments of your suspicious imagination."

"Open the parcel, then, and prove that it's not a present."

"All right," she said defiantly.

Robert switched on the light and watched her while she ripped open the parcel. The cardboard box was full of wood shavings. Nestling in the middle was a round object wrapped in tissue paper with a card beside it. On the card was written, "For all the happy times". Inside the tissue paper was a Victorian glass paperweight enclosing a little country scene of meadow, tree and stream. It was a beautiful example of artistry and craftsmanship, and ignorant though she was of the value of such things, Bridget knew that this must have cost Felix far more than he could afford. For a moment there was a pregnant silence in the car. Then Robert said dryly, "Very touching," pressing the self-starter and drove on. In a few minutes, they had arrived at Bredon Lodge, and after a curt "Goodnight" from Robert, Bridget found herself walking up the drive with the parcel clutched under her arm and the sound of the car dying away on the cold night air.

14

MOMENT OF CHOICE

MOST of the Rainwood family gathered at Bredon Lodge that Christmas, including Lucille and James, so that between helping Gwen and her grandmother with the household chores and discussing the coming visit to the Bahamas with Great-Aunt Lucille, Bridget had little time to brood over the difficult situation that had arisen between her and Robert. She was only thankful that Felix and Susan were in Torquay. It was not until the afternoon of Boxing Day that she was able to escape for a walk on her own and think about her problem, for there was no escaping the fact that Felix had enormously complicated things by his change of attitude. It was a simple matter to demonstrate that she had grown out of the old love while that old love was happily involved elsewhere, but not nearly so simple to convey the truth now that Felix wanted to come into the picture again.

It had been foolish of Felix to give her that present, and yet she was touched by it and could not find it in her heart to blame him for what she interpreted as a farewell memento of things past. Nor could she, in the calm light of day, altogether blame Robert for his false deductions. Knowing all the circumstances, as he did, fate this past week had conspired to put her in a position which must appear to him ambivalent, to say the least. But it distressed her that he would not accept her word that she had finished with Felix.

How exasperating men were, she thought, as she scuffled the dead leaves of autumn that lay thickly on the ground in the beechwood. Why must Felix have nearly broken her heart when he fell in love with Susan, only to have fond hankerings for the past now that he was married and she was free of the old bond? And why did he have to send that parcel through Kit in that surreptitious way, and carefully put no names on the card, when Robert's sharp eyes and alert intelligence were nearby? It would be a relief to go off to the Bahamas and leave the whole business behind, but she wanted desperately to heal the breach with Robert before she went. At the moment he was about as approachable as a moated castle without a bridge. They had exchanged only three sentences throughout the whole of Christmas Day, and his manner had been so irreproachably polite that she had wanted to throw something at him to dent the armour. Perhaps she would find him more approachable when she got back, for he and Kit were due at teatime.

There was a preponderance of young Rainwood cousins at the party that evening, and towards the end of the evening they organised a game of hide and seek in pairs. Bridget partnered the youngest Rainwood, nine-year-old Jonathan, and they were discovered early in the proceedings when Jonathan in his excitement knocked over a standard lamp in the vicinity of their hide-out. Leaving Jonathan to join in the hunt, Bridget tailed Robert out into the hall, where he was searching his coat pocket for a tin of tobacco.

"Not joining in, Robert?"

"Having no girl I want to hide away with in a dark corner, why should I?"

"Then would you come up to my study for a few minutes? I want to talk to you, and this is probably the last chance I'll have before I go away."

"Can't you say it here?"

"No. There's too much traffic."

For a moment she thought he would refuse, then he shrugged his shoulders, and said:

"All right."

In the little gable room at the top of the house, she faced him with wide, troubled eyes.

"I can't go away and leave things like this between us, Robert. You've avoided me all the evening. Are you really going to break off our friendship just because Felix gave me a Christmas present?"

He turned and looked at her, then sat on a corner of her desk and picked up the paperweight.

"It's a nice thing. How attractive you look tonight! A very bright candle for the moths."

"And what does that mean?"

"Are you going to keep this?" he asked, putting the paperweight back on her desk and ignoring her question.

"Yes. I'm sure Felix meant it for a farewell salute to the past, and I shall accept it in that spirit. But I shall make it clear that there must be no more presents."

"Tell me one thing, Bridget. You've been very happy lately. Is it because you're in touch with Felix again after believing that you'd lost him?"

217

"No, no," she said, banging the desk in her vehemence. "I've been happy because I realised that I'd come free of that old entanglement. It was because I was unhappy and lonely in my home life that Felix meant so much to me. Now that my life has changed for the better, I can look back on the past and see it in perspective. I want Felix to be happy with Susan and I've no wish to be in touch with him again. It's over. Quite over. How many times do I have to say it?"

"Then why this present? Something must have happened between you to encourage Felix to do this."

"All right," she said, sighing. "I'll tell you, though I don't like betraying Felix's confidence. When I met him in Latimer's, and it *was* accidental, he was in an unhappy mood, and said things he shouldn't have said. That he would give anything to put the clock back. That I was knitted into his life and always would be there. I'm sure it was only because he was unhappy at being pulled in two because Susan wants him to give up The Monitor and join her father's firm. I told him that I had done with the past, that our paths led in different directions and that I was happy in my new life. He accepted it and said

218

he wouldn't ever mention it again. I believed him, and still do. This present was a goodbye gesture."

"I see. It changes things a bit, doesn't it? To have Felix looking back, too. It could be a messy situation, Bridget. You're aware of that, of course."

"No. The situation is quite clear as far as I'm concerned. This is Felix's goodbye. Mine was said a long time ago. I haven't liked telling you about Felix's private feelings, Robert, and I wouldn't have done if it wasn't so important to me that you should understand what is behind this present."

"I'd feel happier about it if you'd taken a stronger line with Felix. I'm still not sure that he couldn't whistle you back, and if you listen to his trouble with sympathetic eyes and a gentle voice, it's hardly going to discourage him, since he seems to be the weak-kneed type. It hasn't taken him long to start bleating that his wife misunderstands him."

"I'm afraid it hasn't helped, telling you what passed between us at that meeting. You're too intolerant, Robert."

"And you're too soft and woolly-minded, my dear. If Parvey can't support a wife on what he earns from The Monitor and doesn't want to give it up, he should never have married Susan in the first place. But having married her, the last thing he should do is be disloyal to her by complaining to the girl he threw over and trading on the past for her sympathy."

"You sound positively Victorian."

"Maybe. I'm an old-fashioned type. And I haven't finished yet. If you're honest about what you once felt for Felix being over, you should have refused to listen to his bid for sympathy and his disloyalty to his wife, and have told him that he made his choice and has no right now to involve you in any way. And if you're not being honest about your feelings, think carefully before causing trouble in a marriage which has only lasted for nine months and hasn't really had a chance to prove itself yet."

"If I'm not being honest! You think I'm lying?"

"Not wittingly, but I think you may be deceiving yourself, not looking deeply enough."

"You've no grounds for saying that."

"Haven't I? You've never finally cut the bonds between you and Felix. Right from the start, when he threw you over, you still wanted to keep on working for him, and it wasn't until the tongues wagged that you gave up. And it can only have been because he sensed your sympathy, that he spoke as he did to you. And now you keep his present. His photograph still stands on your bookcase. Who are you kidding, Bridget? Yourself?"

"But, heavens, he's an old friend! I don't have to treat him as an enemy, do I?"

"I'm only saying that the situation is one that demands a searching honesty with yourself and a ruthless clear-mindedness about your future dealings with Felix. I've seen too much trouble caused by muddled thinking and a sentimental outlook."

"And where do you come in? Are you going to avoid me, break off our friendship?"

"I've put the situation to you as clearly as I can, and although I've been free with advice in the past, it's reached the stage now where I can only leave the decisions to you."

"But I've told you the truth about my feelings for Felix. What more can I do to convince you?"

"Act on it," he said dryly.

"Why do you take so much convincing,

Robert? What object would there be in my pretending to you?"

"There's comfort in a second-best, perhaps. Someone to fall back on. Or just have fun with. There comes a moment of choice for all of us, you know. One moment when it is possible to see the issues clearly and stop before you're irrevocably involved in something that your reason tells you will be disastrous. There was such a moment for your stepfather, I'm sure. But like most of us, he let wishful thinking persuade him into going on."

"I wish you'd forget my stepfather."

"And have fun?"

"Be happy together without any ghosts."

"It would be very, very easy to have fun with you, Bridget. And if I didn't take you seriously as a person, I'd jump in with the greatest enthusiasm. I think you know that, don't you?"

He held out his hand and she took it. He drew her close and cupped her face in his hands.

"Hair that's a joy, eyes to drown in, and a figure to tempt any man's hand to rove. What do you think I'm made of?"

His kiss left her wide-eyed and shaken.

Then he released her and said gently:

"While the moment of choice is with me, I'll not let my senses stampede me into playing second-best, either to a flesh-and-blood man or a ghost."

"Are you still open to conviction, Robert?" she asked, laying a hand on his arm to detain him as he turned away.

"Yes. But that's up to you now. Have a good time in the Bahamas, and send me a card."

The door closed behind him and Bridget sat down at her desk, feeling suddenly spent. She fingered the glass paper-weight idly as she looked back at the past through Robert's eyes. How all occasions did inform against her, she thought, as she remembered how in her unhappiness she had leaned on Robert's strength to get her through, had not been able to hide from him the extent of her unhappiness. She remembered telling him on that evening of the storm that she could not put Felix out of her heart and didn't wish to. Remembered, too, her stepfather's sneering remarks about constancy and could well imagine what he had told Robert on the same subject. She shivered, thinking that even now her stepfather's hand reached out to remove

223

happiness from her grasp. If only Felix had helped her to make the cut clean. But he hadn't. He had wanted to keep her on The Monitor staff, he was reluctant now to let the old friendship be buried. Perhaps Robert was right and she had not been ruthless enough, but something inside her protested against being brutal to someone who had been as kind to her as Felix had been for all those years of adolescence and after. It shouldn't be necessary. Robert ought to believe her.

She went across to the photograph of Felix and took it out of the frame. She remembered that day so well. It had been hot, and they had sat on the bank of the stream in the shade of an alder tree to eat their sandwiches, and a kingfisher had come to fish while they sat there. A golden summer's day. Why should she not keep a memento of it? Hesitating, she could not bring herself to destroy it, and ended by pushing it into a drawer of the desk, a compromise which Robert would doubtless term woolly-minded. But if to be grateful to a friend for past kindness and happiness were woolly-minded, then she would stay that way. And if Robert demanded such wholesale surrender, would it not be wiser to recognise her moment of choice now and hesitate before losing her heart completely to such possessiveness? He would ask much, and give much, but she, who had submitted for so many years to the dominant personality of her stepfather, wanted to be free of domination. This way and that, her mind turned in an endeavour to clear the path, and beneath it all the recollection of his kiss whispered that her moment of choice had gone, that she was irrevocably committed and had no idea how she was to convince him of that fact.

Perhaps going away would help her to a solution. In a new land of sunshine, blue sea and silvery sand, perhaps her problems would fade and the path be clear. Or perhaps both Felix and Robert would fade and she would be left heartfree to enjoy life as it came, which would be a very pleasant state of affairs, she thought with a clear-sighted dryness of which Robert would approve. A south-sea-island philosophy, that's what I want, she said to herself as she switched off the light and ran downstairs to have a final conference with Great-Aunt Lucille, for they were flying from London Airport on New Year's Day.

15

ANOTHER WORLD, ANOTHER TIME

THEY left London Airport on a day of biting east wind and lowering skies, and emerged from the aeroplane at Nassau some ten hours later to be met by a wave of hot air that made their winter coats seem ludicrous and the need to get into light clothing urgent.

Night had already fallen when they arrived and Bridget's first impressions were a jumble of starry skies, pale sands, the dry whisper of palms in a warm breeze, the gay lights of the town, and a large white hotel overlooking the sea whose style of architecture reminded her of the deep south of Gone With The Wind. As they went in, she glimpsed a dining-terrace with palm-shaded tables looking over green lawn and brilliant flowering shrubs to the sea; an exotic spectacle with its gay lights and calypso band.

Looking round her spacious bedroom after the coloured boy had dumped her cases down with a broad grin, Bridget had to pinch herself to confirm that she was still the same person who less than twelve hours ago had been ducking her head against an icy wind under snow-threatening skies in a land bereft of colour. Her room had its own private bathroom, was beautifully furnished, and had a balcony looking over the sea. With air conditioning, the temperature corresponded to that of a warm summer day at home, and when she had convinced herself that she was not dreaming, she had a quick shower and put on a silk dress. Then, still feeling like Alice in Wonderland, she went out on to the balcony and leaned on the warm stone coping looking across the private beach and the lagoon to the harbour beyond. A cruising liner stood off, its lights ablaze, and in the harbour she could see the outlines of yachts and fishing-boats and schooners. Below her, on the pale sand, she could see a scattering of quaint little thatched straw shelters that would keep off the fiercest rays of the sun. The sea whispered quietly under the night sky, the scent of jasmine wafted to her on the warm air, and the soft rhythm of the calypso music seemed to beat in her blood. And over and above all, the steady rustling of the palm trees in the warm trade wind.

For Bridget, who had never travelled, this sudden transportation to an entirely different world was breathtaking, but that other world was not blotted out, and as she leaned on the balcony, she wished that Robert was there to share these first impressions with her.

As the days passed, it annoyed her that Robert's ghost was with her so much in spite of the absorbing delights that the Bahamas offered, for here, of all places, one should be able to dismiss unsatisfactory love affairs in the enjoyment of the present. With its perfect climate, its blue lagoons, its colourful and cheerful native population and its tropical flowers, it was an ideal background for the enjoyment of the many pastimes, sporting, hedonistic, aesthetic, which the hotels fostered with all the skill and resources at their command. In tourist parlance it was referred to as a holiday paradise, and sampling it as she did under the best conditions at a cost which seemed to Bridget astronomical but which her great-aunt seemed not to consider at all, it was a revelation indeed, and it seemed that Robert's imprint on her life must be deeper even than she had suspected to intrude so often on her absorbing new life.

Her duties were not at all onerous, and she found in the company of Great-Uncle James a source of great pleasure. Whereas Lucille, eight years younger than her brother, gave no impression of old age, and with her smart clothes, business acumen and vigorous personality seemed very much part of the modern world, James at seventy-five was an old man who gave the impression of having contracted out of this world to a serene, twilight country of his own. Tall, thin, with stooping shoulders, he had the same classical features as his sister, Mirabel, but more pinched and sharpened by age, and the same dark blue eyes, but where she looked austere, his face wore a gentle, remote kindliness. And yet, for all his detachment, he seemed to have odd moments of shrewd penetration into the quirks and oddities, fears and hopes, of the human heart.

"My dear," he said to Bridget on the first day, "I know Lucille has appointed you to be my watch-dog, but age and youth can't walk in step and I am perfectly happy pottering about on my own. I shall sketch some of the flowers here, sit in the sun and contemplate. Don't feel tied to me in any way. You are young and active, and must explore and enjoy all these activities, these amazing activities," he added as a couple went past equipped with snorkels for underwater exploring, and James looked over the top of his half-moon glasses the better to observe them, as though they were strange visitors from outer space.

"Well, this morning, like you, I'm quite ready to sit on this terrace and contemplate. We've come a long way since yesterday and I need time to take it in," said Bridget.

"As long as it's not a duty, dear, it will be a pleasure to have your company. Somebody once remarked that a sense of duty is desirable in work, but objectionable in personal relations. I forget who it was. My memory is not what it was, I'm afraid. But it is very true. Very true indeed. Nobody wants to feel that they are the object of somebody's duty. I try to dissuade Lucille from seeing me as a duty, not always with success, I fear. But happily she does not like duty and has the money to pay others to perform it for her and so soothe her conscience, so we are all happy."

It was said without any suspicion of rancour but with a gentle humour which was to become familiar to Bridget over the coming weeks.

"This is a wonderful experience for me. I'm grateful to Aunt Lucille. I've never travelled before."

"No? Let me see, you're Pamela's girl, aren't you?"

"No. That's Alison. I'm Bridget Armadale."

"Armadale?" He turned to look at her, as though doubting his ears.

"Owen's stepdaughter," she said gently.

"Oh, of course. You must forgive me, dear. The family has so many branches that I get confused with the young people. Of course, Lorna's girl. Beautiful woman, your mother. Never saw much of her, but I remember her at Lucy's wedding. She wore a hat of some blue filmy stuff that was perfectly delightful and matched her eyes. I've never forgotten it. Women don't seem to wear pretty hats any more. That was a good many years ago, of course."

"Fifteen."

"As many as that? Dear me. This warmth is really delightful after our cold northern winter. I think I shall have a little nap."

And James, tilting his panama hat over his face, closed his eyes, while Bridget watched the sun-bathers and the swimmers, the white sand and the blue, blue sea, the coconut palms and the fishing-boats, from the shady terrace whose white columns were draped with bougainvillaea and other gaudy flowers which she could not name. Another world. Another time.

Lucille had taken a suite for herself so that she could use the sitting-room as an office, and it was two weeks after their arrival, when Bridget was taking some letters from her there, that she made the announcement which sent Bridget's already high spirits soaring to even more giddy heights.

"I must have Robert in on this. He must negotiate the contract with the solicitors here. An airmail letter will take two or three days to get to him, and then he'll need time to organise things at his end, so I think I'd better telephone him this morning. Let me see, if I get through now, he'll probably be back from lunch. Ask the hotel operator for his number, Bridget, will you?"

With an efficiency which Bridget found impressive, it was no more than a matter of a minute or two before Lucille was speaking to Robert, and Bridget listened with an eager excitement that had nothing to do with Lucille's business project.

"Of course I wouldn't ask you if it wasn't absolutely necessary, my dear boy. I can't miss this opportunity, and I need your professional services . . . That's right . . . Travel first class, and I'll have your accommodation booked here . . . Wait a minute. Why not stay on for a few days after the contract is signed and have a short holiday? Be my guest . . . Of course you can be spared. You must learn to delegate or you'll kill yourself . . . Wire me which flight you'll be on, and we'll meet the plane . . . We're all very well and enjoying ourselves . . . Yes, I know, but I'm paying . . . Young man, you are talking to your great-aunt, though I'll disown you if you ever dare refer to me as such . . . Very well. Goodbye for the present, dear."

Lucille hung up, smiling.

"That young man has a way with him. Doesn't fuss like his dear father did, although he's just as wedded to his responsibilities. Once our business matters are concluded, we must make him relax and enjoy himself, Bridget."

"A splendid idea," said Bridget, who could hardly hide her excitement.

On the day of Robert's arrival, she found herself restless and unable to concentrate on anything but the fact that he would be stepping off the aeroplane at six-thirty that evening. So much, she thought, for her idea that this holiday might put Robert back into perspective. As she ran across the warm sand for her morning swim, she was full of plans for showing him the island, determined to woo him into a holiday mood and make him forget his preoccupation with Felix and past history. Here, surely, in this land of sunshine and colour, they could relax together and enjoy the present. Once business matters were out of the way, she would make him realise who was first in her heart, for she could no longer fail to realise the truth herself. Whether she wished to be heartfree or not, her moment of choice was past, and she was going to do all she could to make Robert's moment of choice a thing of the past, too. So beware, my love, she said to herself as she plunged into the water and swam out with a vigorous crawl stroke that reflected the vitality burning in her that day.

Later, she found Lucille and James reclining on the terrace in long basket chairs, sipping iced drinks, and joined them. The coloured boy brought her a Planter's Punch, and she relaxed, letting the conversation drift over her, hugging her thoughts to herself.

"It's nice to see you resting, Lucille," said James. "You tire yourself with this ceaseless activity. In this climate, you can surely take things more slowly."

"The sun gives me energy. And I like to be active. I bought a delightful blouse in Bay Street this morning. The shops are excellent."

"How odd, to be so devoted to shops."

"When I stop being interested in shops and clothes and the beauty business, I shall be old and finished. I refuse to quit."

"Age is nothing to be frightened of."

"I'm not frightened of it. I just hate it and I intend to fight it all the way."

"Well, you fight it very well, but I sometimes ask myself at what cost."

"My dear James, it's all very well for you to accept it so gracefully. You're interested in plants and birds and the country, and you can enjoy yourself sketching and philosophising. It would bore me into my grave. Frivolous and foolish it may be, but I'm interested in all the trappings and adornments open to women to enhance their glamour and their looks, and I intend to remain interested until I die. And I'd rather buy a bottle of jasmine scent than sketch a jasmine flower."

"Profane woman," said James with a gentle smile, for they both enjoyed teasing each other.

"Well, I haven't done badly out of my interests. They've bought me a comfortable life, so that I only have to do what I'm interested in and am spared the boredom of discomfort and unwanted chores. I funnel my energies where I want them to be funnelled, and that's my recipe for a successful life."

"You always knew what you wanted, Lucille, even when we were children. I remember Mirabel being so cross with you when you insisted on coming to a picnic in your best dress and white buckskin shoes and ducking all the chores for fear of spoiling them."

"Mirabel is often cross with me, I'm afraid. She hasn't your wide tolerance, James. You accept that people are born with different temperaments. Mirabel thinks it's all a question of self-discipline."

"They were happy days, our childhood days. Unfashionable to refer to a happy childhood, but I suppose those early years of the century were the golden ones for the middle classes, and we were lucky to live in the country when Father's pony trap was the only vehicle to come down our lane."

Lucille moved impatiently, not wanting to be reminded of how many years ago it was when they were children, and watched Bridget swing herself off the reclining chair and move to the stone coping. How much she would give to be able to move with such unconscious ease and grace, she thought, as Bridget twined one arm round the stone pillar and leaned there, looking out across the bay. To have a supple body that had no need of corsets, to be able to wear a simple cotton shift and look as cool and graceful as a sylph. What was she dreaming of, this girl with the bright hair and the dark grey eyes and the fair, fine skin which no cosmetics could create? It was proving a success, bringing Bridget, who liked James and was happy to keep an eye on him, besides being an efficient and willing typist. Her judgment had been right, as it usually was. But the girl's presence was a constant and painful reminder of lost youth. How could James accept old age so calmly? Almost welcome it? To her it was an enemy to be fought with all her strength.

Dear Lucille, thought James. She had been a pretty, bright little girl with fair curls and white, even little teeth like a doll's. He could remember her in a sailor suit on her father's knee. The youngest of them, a little spoiled, she had winning ways and an ingenuous expression to mask her determination to mould life to her own desires. And if you were single-minded enough, you could do a good deal of moulding. She had resisted marriage, seeing it as a prison. He wondered if her success in business made up for the lack of husband and children, but if she had any moments of doubt, she had never shown them. How long ago it was, and yet in a way, only yesterday when they had lived in the grey stone house at the end of the lane, with its large, overgrown garden and the stable across the courtyard, where in retrospect the sun always seemed to be shining and he was waving his father off on his rounds, hearing the clip-clop of the pony's hooves grow fainter until the bend hid the trap from sight. And hanging over the gate was the elderberry tree towards which his father, emulating a famous doctor, gravely bowed when passing as a tribute to that tree's valuable medicinal qualities. He could see those moon-coloured blossoms now, gleaming in the dusk of a warm June evening.

And Bridget, separated from Lucille and James by two generations, leaned her head against the warm stone of the pillar and thought not of the past, nor of the present, but only of a few hours hence when Robert would be there, when she could grasp his hand, see his slow smile, hear his deep voice: a tangible presence instead of the ghost that had been walking beside her for the past two weeks.

16

RELUCTANT LOVER

ROBERT spent most of his first few days working in Lucille's sitting-room or cloistered with the lawyers in their Nassau office working on the terms of the contract between Lucille and the owner of the business she was taking over. Bridget did some typing for him, and found him business-like in the extreme.

With the terms agreed, the contract drawn up and signed, he had five days' holiday before he returned.

"Can't you stay longer?" pleaded Bridget on the first free morning when they were alone on the terrace. "I've so much I want to show you, and Aunt Lucille would like you to stay for a week or two."

"Can't be done, I'm afraid. Too busy."

"But to have come all this way and have such a golden opportunity! Surely the business won't fold up if you take a couple of weeks off."

"I've other plans for my holiday. For me, this is a business trip."

"Where are you going for your holiday, then?"

"Ireland."

"It'll be wet and dismal, and here the sun always shines."

"I'm not a sun-worshipper and although this may be your ideal spot, it's not mine. Too commercialised."

"I know. But it's colourful and gay, and there are other islands in the group to be explored."

"My dear, they're all coral islands and the scenery won't vary much. Sunshine, blue lagoons, white sand, palm trees. Unless you like lying on a beach and swimming and then lying on the beach again, five days are ample."

"Oh, Robert!" she exclaimed, exasperated, then was silent as Lucille came out.

"I thought we'd go to lunch at a very nice country club I know, Robert. We'll hire a car and you can drive us round the island afterwards. Suit you?"

"Admirably," said Robert.

During the next three days, Bridget was never alone with him. Lucille, delighted to

241

have a young man to escort her, practically monopolised him, but Bridget felt that Robert was happy with this arrangement and not at all anxious to be alone with her. It was a situation which she had not foreseen, and it was a shattering anti-climax to her hopes and plans. Puzzled by his attitude, she tried to hide her unhappiness and joined in the sight-seeing tours arranged by Lucille with a gay façade. On the third day, when it became apparent that Robert was deliberately avoiding her, pride came to her rescue and she left Robert to Lucille and hired a bicycle to do the exploring which she had hoped to share with him.

She took photographs of fine houses in splendid gardens, of the less stately but not less colourful homes and gardens of the coloured population, of lanes flanked with pink walls over which tumbled masses of bougainvillaea, of one of the picturesque horse-drawn Surreys which had little red curtains at the back, a beaming coloured driver and a horse with a rakish straw hat. It was in a Surrey that she had visualised showing Robert the attractive streets and lanes. Later, she took her camera to the harbour and photographed a liner which had put in that morning, then she wandered round the native market with its piles of fruit and vegetables and its voluble coloured salesmen. She liked the cheerful, casual ways of the Bahamians, and found the children delightful. Perhaps it was the continual sunshine, she thought, that made them seem so happy.

But somehow the enchantment of the first two weeks was lacking. In two days, Robert would be leaving and their old friendship might never have existed for all the notice he had taken of her since his arrival. There was a dinner-dance at the hotel that evening. She wondered whether he would find some way of avoiding dancing with her.

With pride prodding her, she put on a new chiffon dress for the occasion. She had been saving it for a special event. It was the colour of a sapphire, simply cut, with narrow shoulder-straps and a dipping back. With it, she wore a crystal necklace which Lucille had given her on her twenty-fourth birthday, two days after their arrival in Nassau.

But if the beat of the calypso music that night did not bring Robert to his feet, it encouraged a young American who had danced with her a few evenings ago to seek her out again, and halfway through the evening

Robert disappeared. Lucille and James had retired early that evening, so that Robert's defection seemed even more heartless than before. She laughed and chatted with the nice young American until the interval, when a floor show came on. Then she slipped out into the warm night air of the garden, crossed the putting-green and sat down on a seat hidden behind a group of flowering shrubs and looking out over the sea. There, drawing her silk stole round her shoulders, she saw the stars blur in a mist of tears. Then, before she realised what had happened, Robert was sitting beside her.

"I saw you flitting over the green. A rendezvous with your American friend? If so, I'll make myself scarce."

"You've been terribly good at that these past days," she said in a muffled voice.

"You haven't answered my question."

"No rendezvous."

"You're not crying, are you?"

"Of course not. A touch of hay fever. It's the pollen in the air, I expect."

"No doubt. You seem to have taken to the life out here."

"That's not difficult." She summoned up all her resolution to change her tactics. An aggrieved female was a humiliating role to play and not likely to prove rewarding. Moreover, a little demon had reared its head inside her. "Are you afraid of my frivolous influence leading you astray, Robert? You've no idea what delights I'd planned for you but I've a feeling that you've been avoiding me," she said lightly.

"Blue lagoons, starlit nights, calypso music, all the trappings of romance. Highly dangerous."

"Be brave. Risk it. Holidays are different. And you've not much time left."

"Where do we start?"

"Come back and dance," she said, standing up and holding out her hands to him.

"That sounds reasonably safe. All right. But I find the temperature a bit high for dancing."

"We can always come back here to cool off."

"Brazen, aren't you?"

"Two days in holiday mood, Robert. Please give me that. Something to remember."

"Can't your American give you the holiday mood?"

"No. It must be you."

He drew her to him then and she lifted her

face for his kiss. It was some time before they returned to the dance, and then he held her close and there was no opportunity for the American to dance with her again.

It was nearly midnight when they walked back to the seat again. A full moon was sending a silver pathway across the sea and the coconut palms were black etchings against the pale sky.

"It's too much like a glorious Technicolor film," said Robert.

"How hard you are to please."

"Not really. Don't you find an element of slickness, of Tourism with a capital T laid on here?"

"Well, it's a holiday playground to enjoy. You're so serious-minded, Robert."

"I'm too old, perhaps."

"Well, try hard and recapture that first fine careless rapture when you were a gay young man."

"You should take a grain of salt with Kit's descriptions."

But Bridget was sure that she was not the only female to have felt the magnetic pull of Robert's rugged personality, and that the appeal would never have been so strong if he had been an unresponsive man. So much she had learned since falling in love with him.

"Why the resistance, Robert?"

"I told you on Boxing Night."

"How can I convince you? If I had any doubts before, and I don't think I did, I have learned once and for all since I've been here that you come first, that there is nobody else but you now. But if you can't believe it, or perhaps don't care, can't we at least be friends and enjoy ourselves together here?"

"No, because we've passed that stage. As far as I'm concerned, it must be all or nothing. I can't meet you on the light-hearted footing you want."

"I don't want it, but it would be better than behaving as though we're strangers."

"And lead me in up to my neck? I can't play with you, Bridget."

"Nor I with you. But I can't bear to have you here as a stranger. Robert, we have happiness holding out its hands to us. Please don't let the past get in the way. It *is* dead to me, that past. Quite dead. I swear to you. Won't you believe it?"

He took her face between his hands and searched it for a long moment. Then he said quietly, "Yes," and lifted her across his lap.

Her arms went round his shoulders and he blotted out the sky.

She had no knowledge of the passing of time, no awareness of place. To Bridget, this was a new country, a revelation, and she abandoned herself to it with a joyful wonder, giving him the assurance which words had failed to give . . .

"Cold?" he asked. "You shivered."

"Not cold. Who could be cold here? Just wobbly."

He laughed and sat her up as he said:

"Sorry if I was a bit intense. Result of repressions. These last days have been murder."

"Would you have held out?"

"I doubt it. Perhaps. Just. But you looked so . . . radiant, somehow. That vitality of yours. It's such a snare."

"I wasn't feeling at all radiant today."

"Hay fever, in fact. Did it matter so much?"

"Yes. And Robert . . ." She hesitated, then went on, "this is something I've not known before. With Felix, I only knew affection and friendship. There's never been anything like this before. Nothing remotely like it."

He picked up her hand and kissed it gently.

"I believe you. Shall we go for a stroll by the sea? I'm in a melting, buttery mood, a ready victim for moonlight, whispering palms, and all the tourist agent's lyrical promises. You see before you a defeated man."

On her feet, she shook out her rumpled dress.

"That's a seductive number," observed Robert, watching her with pleasure.

"Filmy things are a sure bait for the male. Ask Uncle James, who still remembers my mother's filmy hat at Aunt Lucy's wedding fifteen years ago."

"Well done, Uncle James. I remember a skinny, red-haired brat with large grey eyes and a temper. She improved. Sorry I've broken the shoulder-strap. Will your dress keep up without it?"

"Yes. I can easily sew it on again to-morrow."

He put the stole round her shoulders and arm-in-arm they walked along the track towards the beach.

"Only two days, and there's so much here I want to show you, Robert."

"Such as? I thought Aunt Lucille had been pretty thorough."

"Oh, the odd little corners, like the straw market, and the gardens. And I thought it would be fun to hire a boat and cruise round to find a bay of our own for swimming. And then there are glass-bottomed boats you can go in to see the marine gardens and marvellous fishes. Uncle James and I did that last week. And you must come for a ride in a Surrey with me. I do so want to do that with you."

"The Surrey with the fringe on top. Well, that sounds a pleasant programme. Think we can escape from people anywhere?"

"I know of one quiet little beach. Would you sooner skip the sightseeing and concentrate on that?"

"And each other. Well, maybe we'll fit it all in. Lord, what a landscape! Every romantic cliché present. Still doesn't seem real to me."

"Well, I'm real. Our love is real."

"Stand still while I confirm that."

"Does it seem real now?" she asked after a breathless few moments.

"Beginning to. I think I'll really believe it when I get the same reaction in an English country lane under a grey sky with a chilly wind blowing. I think we'll postpone any serious talk about the future until then, and just enjoy ourselves now. You're in a romantic holiday mood, intoxicated with sunshine, palm trees, and calypso music. Seeing everything through a rose haze."

"It will be just the same in an English lane on a grey day or in Ellarton High Street in a fog. This is no holiday romance and you know it, my cautious lawyer."

"Tell me that when you're home again. Meanwhile, I'm in the mood to yield to your invitation to make the most of these two days together."

And they did. Their wish to be alone was granted more easily than they expected for a slight indisposition kept Lucille to her room for most of the following two days, and James had grown tired of sightseeing and was content to sit on the terrace or in the hotel grounds, sketching or watching the world go by.

In the native market the next day, Robert bought her a conch shell to take home for her study.

"It'll make a nice exotic note on your bookcase," he said, and she knew he was thinking of Felix's photograph.

"So it will. I've nothing on it but a rather repulsive calendar at the moment."

"Good," he said, with a wry little smile. "Now let's go along Bay Street. I saw something there that I'd like for you."

The old Colonial style of architecture in the town and the odd medley of horse-drawn carriages, bicycles and modern cars directed by coloured policemen in pith helmets and smart uniforms had a charm for Bridget which did not stale, and the main shopping street was full of temptations for rich pockets.

Robert was not the kind of shopper to hesitate or ask for approval. He left her outside the jeweller's shop and emerged in a very short time with a small beautifully-wrapped box.

"A bracelet," he said briefly. "Wear it tonight, with that blue dress. I'll take it back with me and pay the duty, and return it to you when you get home. But keep it until I go."

It was a silver bracelet about half an inch wide, with a feathered effect, and in the centre was a heart-shaped cluster of aquamarines. It was beautiful, and she was overwhelmed.

"This will be my most treasured possession, always," she said shakily. "Not only because it's beautiful, but because I know now that you really do believe me, and it seals our compact."

"So it does. Don't let on who gave it to you, though. Not yet. I'd rather we kept it to ourselves until you're home, and we finally seal it in that chilly English lane. Then we'll make it respectable and get a ring. But until then, keep it a secret. Aunt Lucille is too concerned with her tummy just now to notice anything, and Uncle James too intent on his botany."

"Of course. You know, I was so thrilled with this place, but now I'd give anything to be going back on that plane with you tomorrow night. It's going to be six weeks before I see you again. Do you realise that?"

"We'll write."

"It will be March before I'm back, and the crocuses will be out in the garden, and the wood anemones in the copse. And the willows will be showing their catkins in that chilly lane. And suddenly, I'm homesick."

"What? Are the palm trees and tropical seas losing their charm already?"

"I shan't have the right person here to share them with."

"What about that young American who looks so wistfully in your direction?"

"No. I'm a one-man girl. And you're the man. I'll repeat that to you in an English lane, and then I shan't expect to have to make that point again."

He smiled and squeezed her arm as he said:

"Let's dump these packages at the hotel, collect our swimming things and take a carriage across the island to that little bay. We could have a picnic lunch and stay there for the rest of the day. I want you to myself."

Fetching her blue swimsuit from the balcony of her room, she saw Robert come into sight round the corner of the hotel and walk across to their rendezvous on the terrace with his long, unhurried stride. In drill trousers and a white sports shirt, he looked as tanned as though he had been out here for months, and her heart contracted in an ache of loving as her eyes dwelt on his dark face. Powerfully built, there was not an ounce of spare flesh on him, and he moved with the easy grace of a man in good physical trim. The sun must have affected her, as Robert said, to make her feel in such a besotted state. Hurriedly, she stowed her things in a large straw bag, tied a wide-brimmed straw hat under her chin, and ran downstairs as though on wings.

Afterwards it seemed to Bridget that they crammed more into those two days than in the whole of the remainder of her time in Nassau. Suddenly, to both of them, every minute had become precious. Being in love, Bridget found, heightened her perception and enjoyment of the whole range of sights and sounds in that colourful land, and the new country of the senses which Robert opened up to her with an ardour which she had not guessed at, left her with an amazed feeling that she had never lived before.

As their hoarded minutes slipped away and the time for his departure grew nearer, Bridget thought that she could not bear to stay behind.

"You must, my dear," said Robert. "You made a bargain with Aunt Lucille."

"I know. I shall be counting the hours until we leave. And do write often, Robert."

"Of course." He smoothed back the hair from her forehead as she lay on the sand. "This is the last time we'll be alone, so we'd better say our real goodbye here."

"Am I really expected to keep it a secret?

255

I feel it's bursting out of me and must be obvious to all."

"All the same, no admission until after that meeting in an English lane."

"Which lane?"

He thought a moment, then said:

"What about Alder Lane, at the stile on to the heath?"

"Ideal. The blackthorn should be out along there in March. We'll meet there at the very earliest possible moment after we get back, come hail, sleet or thunder. And I'll say to my doubting Thomas that it's just the same there as under the blue skies of the Bahamas, though why you need any more reassuring, I don't know."

"Sun can have a very intoxicating effect on young girls, and there must have been scores of holiday romances that faded afterwards."

"But we haven't just met. We knew before."

"I thought there was some element of doubt, but let's not waste time on an inquest. I'll have to get back to the hotel and pack soon."

Her arms tightened round him, as though fearing to let him go. She wished she could banish that old ghost which still seemed to linger in his mind.

"You've made me so happy, Robert. Happier than I've ever been in my life before. I shall write to you every day and confirm it."

And just then their privacy was invaded by a noisy picnic party and Robert said with a rueful smile as he pulled her to her feet:

"See what I mean about Ireland?"

They said little on their walk back to the hotel. Bridget felt the shadow of his departure like a cold hand on her heart, and tried in vain to chide herself out of this mood with reminders that six weeks was no time at all and that she had enough happiness stored up in her heart to see her over a much longer interval than that. Sensing her drooping spirit, Robert squeezed her arm and gave her a reassuring smile as they arrived back at the hotel.

"Two days to remember. And only the beginning," he said.

17

HOMECOMING

WHEN, as February slipped by, Lucille decided that she needed another few weeks to see that the new business ran smoothly under the salon manageress she had appointed, Bridget felt sick with disappointment, but James came to her rescue by deciding that he had had enough of the sun and intended to fly home by the first available flight.

"I think you'd better go with him, Bridget," said Lucille. "I don't like him travelling all that way on his own, and now that I've got the staff organised at the salon, I don't really need you for typing. You've been invaluable to me, dear," she added hastily. "Quite invaluable."

"It's been a wonderful experience for me. I'll always be grateful to you," said Bridget.

Lucille, her mind very much wrapped up in her new business, left Bridget to make the travelling arrangements, and a cancellation enabled her to get tickets for a flight back two days earlier than they had originally planned. It would mean that she would now have to wait two days after she arrived home before she could see Robert, who had purposely brought forward a business trip to Edinburgh so that he could be back by the first of March to meet her in Alder Lane, but she was as anxious now to get back as was James.

"The sun," declared James in his reedy voice, "can be very monotonous, and I long for cool nights. Haven't slept at all well here. The smell of rain will be quite welcome, and spring will be on the way now. Our countryside in spring is not to be beaten anywhere, and when we grumble at our weather, we must always remember that it is the climate which gives us our beautiful countryside."

"I do. I wonder if the primroses are out yet. They're so lovely in the woods behind Melbridge church," said Bridget, and went off to send Robert an airmail letter with the news.

They were both hard put to it not to seem too eager to be gone.

They arrived at London Airport early on the Thursday morning, and were met there by Lucille's chauffeur with her Bentley car and

Charles Rainwood with Bryn and the shabby old Austin. James insisted on being driven straight home to the Sussex house which he shared with Lucille, and Bridget knew that he was tired of the pressure of other people and wanted to be at peace, alone, for a spell.

Driving back to Bredon Lodge, she looked at the country around her with fresh eyes. She seemed to have been away for a lifetime and to have come back to a different world. A world dominated by Robert. In two days, she thought, she would see him, and she could hardly bear to wait.

Her welcome home could not have been warmer.

"We've missed you more than we can say," said Mirabel, embracing her. "And how well you look, dear! This is a cold day for you after your spell in the sun."

"I don't feel it. I think I must have stored up the sun inside me and now it's warding off the cold. It's good to be home, though."

"And it's good to hear you say that, Bridget."

There was much to talk about, films to be shown, postcards to be passed round, family news to be exchanged, unpacking to be done. The day passed quickly. In her room that night, Bridget stood by the window looking out over the shadowy garden beneath a fitful moon that seemed to be playing hide and seek with the clouds. One more whole day, and then it would be Saturday. He had said eleven o'clock at the stile, but she would be there earlier so that she could watch the heath and see him coming.

The next morning brought her a disturbing letter from Felix.

Dear Biddy,

I saw you driving through Ellarton this morning with Mr. Rainwood, and am glad you are back. Hope you had a good time.

I'm in trouble and need your help. You're the only person I can trust, and as we're such old friends, I'm counting on you. It's urgent, or I wouldn't be bothering you the moment you get back, like this. I shall be in the lane behind Melbridge Church at seven-thirty this evening. I must see you, Biddy. You are my last chance. Please come, for old times' sake. In haste.

Felix

The little grey church with its squat tower looked pale and peaceful in the moonlight

261

that evening as Bridget took the path through the churchyard. The old yew trees cast black pools of shadow and the only sound to break the stillness of the night was an owl hooting from the woods beyond. As she climbed the stile into the lane, a figure detached itself from the hedge and came towards her.

"Biddy! I knew you wouldn't let me down. I've got the car just off the road here."

He took her arm and shepherded her to the car, which he had parked in the gateway to a farm.

"Hop in. Too chilly to stand about."

In the front seat of the car, she turned to him.

"Felix, is it wise to call me in on whatever's the trouble? You know how Susan would hate it."

"There was no one else I could turn to. You don't have to help me, Biddy. But if all those years of friendship mean anything to you, or ever meant anything to you, please listen."

"Of course. Go on."

"I'm in a hole for money. I owe a chap a hundred and fifty pounds. I borrowed it to meet some bills of Susan's and some racing debts. Like other idiots who get in difficulties, I thought I could get out by gambling, knowing absolutely nothing about racing and listening to some chump who professed to be in the know. The man I borrowed it from can't give me any more time to pay and he's threatening to go to Sue's father if I don't pay him tonight. I don't blame him. He can't see why I won't borrow from my father-in-law, seeing that he's rolling in it, but if I do that, I'm sunk."

"Surely Uncle Peter would help you."

"Rather. That's what he's waiting for. He'd help me all right. On his terms. That I go into his business. He's got a splendid job all lined up for me, in his publicity department. Getting out a chatty news sheet once a month and supervising the advertising. At a salary four times my present one, with prospects of becoming a director at an early date. All for Susan's benefit, of course. Can you imagine me whipping up enthusiastic paragraphs about our January sales bargains or the latest playtime casuals? I'd die rather than ask him for help."

Bridget, shocked by his bitter tone, could only say:

"I'm so sorry, Felix, but if The Monitor is such a bad paying proposition, couldn't you get into Fleet Street? You're a first-class journalist."

"I've a chance of salvaging The Monitor and making it a paying proposition. Our rival county magazine wants to join forces. Hugh Downing's the new owner. I used to know him in the old days, when we were both reporters on the local paper. I'm meeting him next week for a discussion. We'd halve our overheads and double our circulation if we joined forces, but I simply must get hold of enough money to tide me over this crisis. I've barely enough to pay the wages next week. If I could borrow two hundred pounds, it would pay my debt and give me a breathing space. With any luck, the future could be a lot easier. I hate asking you, Biddy. But you understand what my work means to me, and you're the only person I can trust to keep this secret. I know your stepfather only left you a few hundreds, but if you could possibly raise this loan, I'll pay it off within the year, I promise. If I can't make a go of this amalgamation, then I'll have to get another job or yield to the Rainwood pressure, but give me this one chance to keep The Monitor going."

"All right, Felix. I can make it, I think."

"My dear . . . I've no right . . ." He stumbled and broke off, taking her hand.

He was in a strained, emotional mood which she found difficult to handle.

"There's no need to say any more," she said gently. "You made my life bearable all those years. I'll gladly help. But, Felix, don't involve me in your married life. This is a business arrangement between us. The old friendship belongs to the past. You won't forget that, will you?"

"No, my dear. If that's your wish."

"It is, and must be. I haven't got my cheque book with me. You say you must have it tonight?"

"Yes. I'm meeting Bill at our local tonight. Can you get your cheque book now and slip out again without any questions being asked?"

"Yes. I'll be back in twenty minutes."

She took the short cut and slipped into the house by the side door. She met nobody, but heard voices from the drawing-room as she ran quietly up to her study. It sounded as though some visitors had arrived. Creeping down, she hurried through the kitchen and out again, closing the door quietly behind her. In the car, she made the cheque out to

Felix's friend for the hundred and fifty pounds, and another to Felix for fifty.

"I can't thank you enough," he said. "I'm already in your debt for so much that I'm ashamed to ask for this too. But it will be repaid. For everything else, I'll never be able to repay you. Not one girl in a thousand would do what you've done this evening, without reproaches. Loyalty like that is rare in this world, I assure you."

"Don't worry about it. I hope the amalgamation goes through and is a success. Now I must go."

"I know I don't have to say this, Biddy. But you won't let a word of this leak out anywhere, will you? The Rainwood tribe is so closely knit that the grapevine works wonderfully, and if any word got out about this to anyone, I bet it would reach my father-in-law's ears within the hour. And then I'd be sunk."

"Nobody shall know of it, Felix. You have my word. Don't get in touch with me again, though. Not on your own. Your world is a different one from mine now. Goodbye. And good luck."

"Bless you. Lord, how I wish things had been different!"

"That's foolish," she said gently.

He caught her arm as she turned to slide out of the car, and drew her face between his hands, he kissed her and said:

"Goodbye, my dear Biddy."

Walking back, troubled by this meeting, hoping that things would get smoother for Felix now, she was surprised to hear the church clock strike nine, and quickened her steps. Her grandparents would be thinking that her stroll that night was somewhat prolonged.

"Oh, there you are, dear," said Mirabel when Bridget joined them in the drawing-room. "What a pity you've just missed Robert."

"Robert? Is he back? I thought he was returning on the sleeper from Edinburgh tonight."

"He got away this morning, after all. He arrived soon after you'd gone out. I must say it was nice of him to come here as soon as he got back. I think he was disappointed at not seeing our returned traveller. I told him you'd only slipped out for a stroll and he waited a bit, then said he'd have to go. He was feeling a little tired after the journey and cramming a lot of work into the week. He seemed a bit edgy, I thought. Most unusual for Robert. He works too hard."

"I'm sorry I missed him."

Gwen came in just then with the usual evening pot of tea, and Bridget began to talk about the life in Nassau, not wanting to go any further into her long absence that evening. Behind her deep disappointment at missing Robert was a lurking uneasiness, and she wondered whether to telephone him that night, or whether to wait now until their planned meeting. He would presumably have left a message or would telephone her if he wanted to alter it. He had been travelling all day, and must have come on here almost straight from his journey. If only he had waited a little longer! But perhaps she preferred, after all, to meet him on their own, away from other eyes when her feelings would need no masking. It was getting late now, and he would be tired. She decided not to telephone, but to keep their first greetings for the appointed hour.

March came in with a fine, breezy day, and as Bridget got off the bus at Alder Lane that morning, she felt like dancing with happiness and eagerness. Her disappointment of the previous evening was swept aside and the heady air of spring intoxicated her already effervescent spirits. In the sheltered lane, the blackthorn was just coming into flower, and the hazel catkins were shedding pollen on the wind. She reached the stile fifteen minutes too early, and sat on top of it, facing the heath, her eyes watching the oblique footpath which led from Oakdene. The wind blew softly in her hair and the sun felt warm on her face. A solitary rider was crossing the heath at a steady trot. When he reached the wide grassy gallop, he shook the horse into a canter and disappeared round the bend behind a cluster of birch trees. Idly, she watched a hen blackbird collecting pieces of dead bracken and grass for a nest. It flew off towards a thicket of gorse and hawthorn. High up above, out of sight, the song of a lark rippled on the air.

Bridget shifted. The bar of the stile was getting hard. It was ten minutes past eleven, and Robert was not yet in sight. The blackbird was back again, tugging at a long piece of wiry grass. Then her heart jumped as she saw a man's figure on the path, but as he drew nearer she saw it was an elderly man who turned off on a side track. A few minutes later, two young girls came along with a lively sealyham at their heels. They smiled as Bridget got off the stile to let them climb over it. The sealyham let out a yelp of excitement and went streaking down the lane, followed by the girls, laughing and chattering. Their voices died away, leaving no sound but the lark and the wind in the hedgerow trees.

She waited there until twelve, hunched up, getting stiff and chilly, and yet strangely unable to move. She seemed to be caught in a trance, suspended in time, as though by ignoring the passing of the minutes she could keep at bay the realisation that Robert was not coming. When at last she clambered back and down again into the lane, she was so stiff that she almost fell. Waiting for the bus to Melbridge, a bleak numbness still seemed to rule her mind.

Gwen came out into the hall as she was walking upstairs.

"Miss Bridget, I'm so sorry, but Miss Mellon left this package for you just after breakfast this morning. Bryn brought it in and left it in the kitchen without telling me about it, and I only found it just after you'd gone out."

"Miss Mellon?" said Bridget stupidly.

"Yes. Mr. Robert's housekeeper," said Gwen, giving her a curious stare.

Bridget pulled herself together.

"Of course. I'm day-dreaming. Thanks, Gwen."

In her bedroom, she opened it. The box contained the bracelet Robert had bought her. With it was a note.

Sorry I returned too soon last night. I saw you on my way home, but it didn't seem an opportune moment to interrupt you.

Keep this as a memento of your holiday fun in the sun.

Robert

18

A QUESTION OF TRUST

"I'M sorry if Robert is busy, Miss Mellon, but I must see him this evening. Tell him I'll wait until he can spare a few minutes."

Bridget leaned back in the armchair with an air that intimated that she would sit there until Doomsday if necessary. Miss Mellon looked a little embarrassed and went off with her message. For a whole week, Bridget had tried to see Robert without success. This time, she was not going to be put off.

He came in quietly, closing the door behind him, and his face was as grim as an arctic winter. She half rose, then sank back in the chair. This was far removed from the meeting she had dreamed about for the past weeks.

"Well, Bridget, what do you want with me?"

She stared at him, unable to believe that he could be so changed from their last meeting.

"You don't think I was going to let things rest with that cruel little note you sent me, do you?"

"You would be well advised to. I thought it let you down pretty lightly."

"You saw me with Felix that night."

"Yes. It was unlucky for you that I was foolish enough to be too eager to wait until Saturday when I saw a chance of getting back a bit sooner. I thought I recognised Felix's car on my way over but I passed too quickly to register anything very definite. When Grandma told me you had gone out for a short walk, I waited, but I had an inkling then. When I drove back, I had a closer look. Felix should have pulled the car farther off the road or turned it round. It was a very cosy picture."

She remembered the car passing; its lights had swept over the goat willow by the farm gate and she had noticed the silvery buds over Felix's shoulder, appreciating their fairy-like appearance in that sudden light even as Felix kissed her.

"He was saying goodbye. It was an urgent business matter he had to discuss with me," said Bridget desperately, realising how thin the truth sounded, and realising, too, for the first time, just how disastrous that meeting with Felix could prove.

"Spare me such feeble excuses, Bridget. You may have amused yourself with me by those blue lagoons, having fun, but don't treat me as though I'm an idiot, please," he said bitingly.

"It may sound feeble, but it's the truth. It was a business matter we were discussing."

"What business?"

"I gave my word to Felix that I wouldn't disclose it to anybody. It concerned The Monitor."

"And the fond embrace? Just oiling the business? You've got a nerve, I must say, coming here with such flimsy excuses. You've never stopped loving Felix Parvey, and you'll run to his every whistle. He didn't waste much time whistling for you this time. He even beat me to it, and I was keen enough, heaven knows!"

"You can't believe that I was pretending in Nassau, Robert. That it was just a game to me. You can't!"

"A game? Perhaps not. It could have been compensation you were taking for defeat and frustration elsewhere. A feeling that a second string would be pleasant. I've kept my temper so far, Bridget, but I think you'd better go now, because I can't guarantee to keep it much longer. You cheated me, and I don't like being cheated."

"That's not true. I love you, Robert. Felix is no more than a friend, was never any more. Why should I lie about it?"

"Why? Well, Felix does happen to be married, and whatever you two may do on the sly, if marriage is a desirable goal, you'll have to look elsewhere. And a nice credible husband would provide a good smokescreen, after all."

"You think I'm as low as that? After all these months of friendship, you can think that about me?"

"I put my cards on the table. I told you that I'd never play second best to another man, and that was why I was keeping off. I was honest with you. And you deliberately invited me on, swore that Felix meant nothing to you. Then, almost immediately you get home, you're meeting him secretly in a dark lane, kissing in a car, knowing that I'm safely in Edinburgh. Felix is a married man, with a wife who is already jealous of you, with good cause, it seems, and you risk all the trouble that could ensue to be with him for a few hours. And you look up at me with wide eyes and say 'How can you think me so low?' "

"It was a business meeting," said Bridget, banging the arm of her chair in despair. "You happened to see Felix saying goodbye in a way I couldn't stop and didn't seek. We had done nothing but talk business before then."

"Then why didn't you do it in his office, openly, instead of lurking in a quiet lane in his car? You must think me an imbecile."

"It had to be confidential and it was urgent."

"For pity's sake," said Robert, putting his hands to his head, "don't try me too hard. I hate violence, but, so help me, I'm beginning to feel violent now. Please go, and keep out of my way. No man likes being made a fool of, but it's not just my pride that's damaged. I really cared. You were very successful there. I don't intend to burn my fingers twice, though."

"And do you think I didn't care?" she asked passionately. "Do you think I was acting in your arms out there? Am I so experienced that I could act that well?"

"I believed you then," he said bitterly, and turned away to the window, staring out of it, his hands clenched behind his back.

"If I could prove to you that it was a business matter we were discussing, would you believe that Felix's kiss meant no more than I said?"

"Could you prove it?" he asked ironically.

"I shall ask Felix to release me from my promise to tell nobody and make an exception of you."

"You see. You'll ask Felix. Always Felix first. Remember your stepfather's words? I've never forgotten them. You're like your mother. Felix lives in your heart and mind as your father lived in hers. If we married, Felix would eat at our table, live in our house, sleep in our bed. But your mother, at least, came to the point where she wouldn't deny it. I'm not a candidate for the same kind of torture as your stepfather endured."

"You said you were open to conviction about Felix, but you're not, are you? You've made up your mind that I love Felix and my denials are useless."

"Good heavens, look at the evidence!"

"I know. But when people love you, you expect them to believe that you're not a liar. No matter what the evidence, I should believe you because I know you're not a liar. I shouldn't love you if you were."

"The best I can think is that you're not a deliberate liar, that you only deceive yourself, won't admit the truth to yourself. And that's stretching it a bit in the light of the evidence," he said grimly, but she felt that his reason was beginning to govern the violence that had threatened.

"Do you think I would try to trap you into a marriage which would be hell for all of us? Do you think I haven't enough intelligence to know what an unhappy marriage is like? I lived with it in my childhood and I've thought a lot about it since. Do you think I would want history to repeat itself?"

"Women want marriage and children. Most of them. It's a biological urge not governed by reason. And I might seem a passable choice, especially as the family connections would enable you to keep in touch with Felix."

There it was again. The violent bitterness in the tail.

"Don't let jealousy corrode your reason, Robert. I know appearances are against me. They always have been, where Felix is concerned. I can only say, as I've said so many times before, that he was a childhood friend, that it never grew to be anything more, and that although I was unhappy to lose that friendship at a time when it was all I had, the feeling I had for him was never love. I didn't know what that was until you taught me. And somehow, against all the evidence, I feel you should know that. But if I can repair any of the damage by telling you more about my meeting with Felix that night, I will. I can't bear you to think that I would hurt you like this."

"It's not uncommon in the battle of the sexes. I've been lucky in keeping clear until now, and all experience is useful, I guess."

His voice was hard now and she knew that further efforts would avail her nothing.

"I'll go now. If I can't make things right between us, Robert, I shall return the bracelet. It sealed a contract. If the contract's broken, and you think I'm a cheat, I shan't want it."

"The paper-weight will be a reminder of a happier relationship, no doubt. If Felix doesn't want to be found out, may I suggest that you warn him to be a little more careful about the choice of a rendezvous? It's better to go on foot. A car is always difficult to hide, and is easily recognised."

"Because you're hurt, you want to hurt me,

but if it's any satisfaction to you, nothing can hurt me as much as sitting on that stile last Saturday waiting for someone who didn't come. Your package and the message didn't get to me until I arrived back. It had been in the kitchen, overlooked. I waited until twelve. I'd been counting the hours and the days for so long. I'd been thinking of nothing else ever since you left Nassau. So you punished me all right."

"Then I suggest we call it quits, but at least you didn't find me making love to another girl."

Bridget looked at him helplessly. His dark face was masked now with a laconic expression that put an insuperable barrier between them. He was a man who could always ride his emotions on a tight rein. Even on that morning, when she had sensed a frightening savagery in him, he had kept control. In the Bahamas she had discovered a passionate depth of feeling behind the calm, assured manner which Robert always wore. For all his rational approach to life, his keen intelligence, he was no cold intellectual, as her stepfather had been. But, at whatever cost, he would always have the strength of mind to rule his heart and would never compromise.

Blindly, she shook her head and left him. He made no attempt to see her out and she fumbled at the door-latch with a shaking hand and blurred eyes.

She wrote to Felix that evening.

Dear Felix,

It is my turn to ask a favour of you now. Will you release me from my promise to tell nobody about our transaction and let me make an exception of Robert? He saw us in the car the other night and drew the wrong conclusions. In Nassau, we discovered that we loved each other and were going to be engaged on my return. Unless I can explain what happened the other night, everything will be finished between Robert and me.

I am keeping to the bald facts because the whole business has made me so unhappy. You can rely absolutely on Robert's integrity and discretion. It will go no further than him. But in view of all that has gone before, and which I won't weary you with, I think he has a right to know the truth.

Hope the amalgamation is going through successfully.

Biddy

His reply came by return.

My dear Biddy,

I'm sorry, I can't agree to what you ask. Robert is a true Rainwood and has no liking for me or I for him. I blame him for a lot of the talk that went on about us before, and if he knew about our transaction, it would be round the family in a trice and Sue's father would have me where he wanted me.

If Robert doesn't trust you, he's a fool, and you're far too good for him, anyway.

You did give me your promise, my dear, and I know you'll stick to it. If Robert lets this make any difference, he doesn't deserve you and you'll be better off without him. Personally, I should be sorry to see you marry him. Too sure of himself for my taste, and, like all the Rainwoods, bent on having his own way always. If you think you owe me anything for all those years of our friendship, and I don't admit that you do—you gave me far more than you took—don't sell me down the street to Robert Rainwood. It would be disastrous for me, Biddy. Trust my judgment there. You are altogether too trusting yourself. I only hope R.R. won't start the gossiping about us again. I wouldn't put it past him. But even that sort of gossip would do less damage at this stage in my affairs than the revelation that I was broke and had borrowed money from you. After all, it's no crime to have a friendly chat in a car.

The whole object of the operation will be nullified if your generosity gets out, Biddy. I am seeing Hugh Downing again tomorrow.

Thank you again, my dear, for your loyalty and help. And I must be frank and say I'd be relieved to know that an engagement between you and R.R. was ruled out. I don't think for a moment that he would make you happy, and you deserve happiness if anyone does.

Yours ever,
Felix

Bridget sat at her desk fingering the glass paper-weight as she read this letter for the third time. Felix was wrong about Robert. Was it jealousy that made him so anxious to denigrate him or was it merely part of a general animus against the Rainwood family because of the pressures that his wife and father-in-law were putting on him? At that moment, her mood was one of anger against both the men in her life. Robert for not believing her in spite of the circumstantial evidence against her, and Felix for disregarding completely in his own interests her declared love for Robert. But she had given her word, and something in her rebelled at having to prove to Robert that she had not cheated him.

For the rest of that day, she worried at it, wavering from a passionate desire to put things right with Robert at all costs to an angry wish to be rid of the pangs and complexities of love, to be free of men who had played such havoc with her life during the past year. It seemed to her that her stepfather's hatred of Armadale blood lived on to deny her happiness. More than anything, it was his example and his strictures about her that had paved the way for Robert's attitude.

When she went to bed that night with a raging headache and unhappiness like an icy weight on her heart, she had still come to no decision about what she should do.

The next evening, her mind made up, she packed up the bracelet and went to see Robert. This time, Miss Mellon asked her to go into Robert's study, where she found him at his desk surrounded with papers. He knocked his pipe out on an ashtray as she sat down in the chair he indicated, feeling like a patient consulting a specialist.

"Well, Bridget?" he asked.

"I wrote to Felix asking him to release me from my promise to tell nobody about the subject of our business discussion," she said, as though reading out the minutes at a board meeting, "but he refused."

"I'm not surprised," said Robert calmly.

Their mood had hardened since their last meeting, and they eyed each other with a wariness bordering on hostility.

"He didn't think you were to be trusted," said Bridget coldly, allowing her anger to dictate to prudence. "Forgive me if trust is beginning to sound a dirty word. It's something I can't expect from you, obviously, and perhaps it's as well to have found that out before we committed ourselves to an engagement. I can't think any marriage would stand much chance if one partner distrusted the other."

"I agree. It would be a farce. I don't fancy myself in the role of the hoodwinked husband, though, with the other chap always just slipping out of the back door as I come in at the front."

"How dare you say that?"

"Don't get excited. Stick to facts, not emotions. You're too apt to think with your emotions, and some very muddled results they come up with."

"Have you no insight into feelings, Robert? Are you quite unable to recognise sincerity when you see it? I couldn't have shown you my heart any plainer than I did in Nassau. You really think that was acting?"

"Oh, it was probably sincere at the time. Exciting, enjoyable, flattering. I'm no hypocrite. I enjoyed it, too. But it was more than fun to me."

"And to me."

"Then you must be satisfied with one at a time," said Robert calmly.

"Sometimes I hate you," she declared passionately.

"I dare say. It's infuriating of me not to fall in with your pattern for an enjoyable triangle. I so nearly did. If I hadn't returned a day earlier than expected, we would have been snugly engaged by now. Unless your organisation with Felix improved, though, there was always the likelihood of my finding out. You're neither of you, if I may say so, very clever at covering your traces."

"How cheap can you be?"

"As cheap as you were in Nassau. I'm tired of this topic. It goes round and round like a toy horse at a fair. All I hope is that you won't provoke a scandal in the family. It could hurt a lot of people. I think Felix is more to blame than you. He wants two strings to his bow, too, but when he married Sue he promised to keep to one and it's barely a year since their wedding. I'm not going to warn you again. I've done enough of that in the past and it's obvious that you pay no attention. If there is trouble, you'd get flayed by the family, though. The Rainwoods are a clannish lot and very conventional in their moral outlook, I'm afraid."

"I don't need your warning because there's nothing between Felix and me that would shock a Victorian grandmother."

"Presents, secret meetings in a dark lane, declarations from Felix that he'd give anything to put the clock back because he'd made the wrong choice, a sympathetic ear from you. Would any Victorian grandma approve of that?"

"You make it sound sinister. It wasn't like that at all."

"Heaven help me to keep patient! Can you really be so green? Whatever the nature of

287

your association with Felix this past year, innocent or not, you should have finished with him finally once he was married, and you know it, you must know it."

"Must I be hostile to an old friend, treat him as an enemy, because he's married? I never sought him out. I've only seen him a few times since his marriage."

"Be that as it may, even now you're dancing to his tune. Keeping his secrets. And I may have a dirty mind, but I really find it hard to believe that they're business secrets."

"I would like to tell you about it, but I made a promise. If our relationship has to be built on breaking my word to a friend I owe a lot to, then it's not worth much. What can I build on disloyalty? I ask for your loyalty and trust."

"And a naïveté I lost in my teens," he said dryly.

Perhaps it was the detachment in his voice, the twist of his mouth, that set her trembling with anger. In a minute, she thought, we shall be fighting. I want to use physical violence, to hammer at him. And this is the man I love. This immovable block of granite. She pulled the package out of her bag and flung it on to the desk.

"Here's your bracelet. You've destroyed something that could have been so good, Robert. You think it's because I've cheated you, lied to you, let you down. Whatever the circumstances, I can't forgive you for believing that of me. Goodbye."

She ran out of the room, not trusting herself to say another word, and fled into the welcoming darkness of the night.

19

A BAD JOKE

THE dining-room of The Crown Inn at Oakdene was full at lunchtime that Saturday. Robert, at a corner table, had just given his order and was reading the paper when a voice hailed him.

"Hullo, stranger."

Robert looked up. The voice belonged to a beefy young man with a pale, rather pudgy face and a wide grin.

"Bill Brent. Well, well. How's life?"

"A bit bleak at the moment. Suffering from a hang-over. Fred tells me he won't have a table free for at least half an hour. Care to be a good Samaritan and let me share yours?"

"Sure," said Robert, who had never felt less sociable in his life, but who nevertheless had a liking for Bill Brent dating from the days when they were the opening pair for the Oakdene Cricket Club.

"Come here often?" asked Brent, settling himself in the chair opposite Robert.

"Most Saturdays. You're putting on weight, Bill. Sooner the cricket season starts, the better."

"Not playing any more. Taken up golf instead. Got a crack on the knee a couple of seasons back and it's played me up ever since. Golf suits my advancing years better now. You keep pretty trim. In fact, you look disgustingly healthy to my jaded eyes today."

They chatted about cricket and local affairs until they reached their coffee.

"Black and strong for me, Fred," said Brent to the waiter.

Robert eyed him with a faint grin. His companion had only toyed with his lunch and winced now at a loud burst of laughter from a party in the corner.

"What caused the hang-over? You're a pretty seasoned type."

"It must be old age. We had a bit of a binge at the club-house after a competition in which yours truly didn't do at all badly."

"Meaning you won?"

"Yes. Now I'm paying for my folly in mixing them with a shocking head, a worse mouth, and the knowledge that I've put my clumsy foot in it properly. They say confession's good for the soul, and I'd like a spot of advice. You know Felix Parvey, of course, since he married your cousin."

"Yes. Not that I have much to do with him."

"Decent chap. Editor of The Monitor. I got to know him some years ago when he was on the local rag and reported our cricket matches. Gave us quite a bit of welcome publicity in our struggling days, if you remember."

"Go on," said Robert, accepting a cigarette.

"Well, all this is strictly confidential, but since you're a member of the family, so to speak, you might be able to offer a few words of wisdom. That legal mind of yours has a detachment that I need just now. My own head feels as though it's stuffed with cotton wool. Lord, what a laugh that woman's got! Never marry a loud-voiced woman, old son. They're always the worst. Seems to go with a bossy nature."

"I'm in no danger."

"Well, to get down to brass tacks. Felix was a bit tight for cash a few weeks ago. I'd just had a win with a premium bond and I was flush. I lent him a hundred and fifty quid. He said he'd be able to pay it back at the end of the month. Well, no need to go into details, but it dragged on and then I needed the cash to buy a car which a pal of mine was letting go dirt cheap for a quick sale. I got a bit annoyed with Felix for not tapping his father-in-law, since he's stiff with money, and I said if he wouldn't, I would, since I wanted that car and I thought someone else might snatch it up any moment. I gave him a deadline. Well, he came up with a cheque from a friend, and that was that. I should have kept my silly mouth shut after that. The affair was closed. But last night, we were all merry, cracking jokes, you know how it is, when Felix's name came up. Something about a series of golf articles that had appeared in The Monitor. We'd been talking about girl friends, and I, like a prize chump, had to make some footling joke about Parvey's out-standing prowess with the fair sex since he'd actually got a bird who paid his debts instead of running them up. Something like that. It sounded rather bright at the time. Of course, if I'd been sober, I'd never have dreamed of saying anything like that.''

"Go on," said Robert grimly.

"Well, how was I to know that Parvey's pa-in-law was at the bar just behind us? I knew

293

he was a member, but he seldom stays on in the bar. I didn't spot him until a few minutes later, when the jokes about it had developed a blue tinge, as you can imagine, and I hoped he hadn't heard any names. But he cornered me afterwards and asked me what foundation I'd got for such statements about his son-in-law. That pulled me up, I can tell you. But the only thing I could think of to get me out of the hole was to pretend to be too fuddled to know what he was talking about. He looked pretty disgusted, I can tell you, but he went off without saying any more. Now I've probably landed old Felix in the devil of a mess, and I could cut my tongue out."

"Did you mention who the girl friend was?"

"That's the trouble. I can't remember."

"How did you know it was a woman's cheque?"

"I recognised the name, B. L. Armadale, and it was a woman's handwriting. It was that red-head who used to go around with him. I believe she worked on The Monitor at one time. I only met her once, years ago. Rather a nice kid with big grey eyes. Now I'm blessed if I know what to do. I feel a regular heel. Enough to make me go teetotal. Can you suggest anything that might help? I like old Felix. Wouldn't make trouble for the lad for the world. Wasn't serious when I said I'd go to his pa-in-law for the cash if he didn't pay. Just wanted to stir him up. I was a bit peeved because he'd led me to understand that the money was only needed to tide him over for a week or two, whereas he was obviously in the deuce of a hole. I'm not in a position to make long-term loans."

"Well, you're a prize ass, I must say," was Robert's unconsoling comment. "Slander actions have been brought for less."

"I know, old son. You don't have to tell me what a prize ass I am. But it was only a joke. You know what it is with a gang of chaps at a celebration. I don't know whether to warn Felix, send a written apology to Mr. Rainwood and say it was all poppycock, or what."

"I think the damage is done. You'd better say no more about it until you see if there's any sequel. You might have thought of the girl's reputation if you didn't care about Parvey."

"But it was only a joke. Not meant seriously at all. And I may not have mentioned the girl's name. I certainly didn't intend to, and I don't think I did, but I can't be sure.

It's all a bit dim," said Brent, leaning his head on his hand as though it would not stand up on its own any longer.

"Well, although I could wring your neck, because I happen to know the girl in question, I'll see if I can do anything to mend the situation. I'm glad you told me. There may be time to stop the rot."

"Do you think so? How? I'd do anything to help. Recant, say I was muddling Parvey up with someone else. Anything."

"I don't think that would convince my Uncle Peter, who is a pompous ass in some ways but not dim-witted. This happened last night, you say? I'd better not waste any more time telling you what I think of you, Bill. Remind me to continue in the same strain when I see you next."

"Have a heart. I'm wearing sackcloth and ashes, I can tell you. I'll be no end grateful if you can paste over my gaffe somehow, though I'm blessed if I see how. You're a clever old so-and-so, though, and I'm darned glad I ran into you today. Keep me informed. Where are you starting?"

"With the person you've damaged most, of course. Bridget Armadale," said Robert flintily, and signalled for his bill.

Tapping his finger impatiently on the desk while the telephone rang at Bredon Lodge, Robert was eventually answered by his grandmother's formal voice.

"You've been engaged a long time, Grandma. How are you?"

"Very well, dear."

"Is Bridget there?"

"No, she's gone to the village to post a parcel."

"When are you expecting her back?"

"I'm not sure. She said she might go for a walk over the heath. Robert . . ."

"What is it, dear?"

"Just before you rang, I had Uncle Peter on the telephone making all sorts of dreadful accusations about Bridget and Felix. He's coming over straight away to see her, and I'm very worried. He seems beside himself with rage, and talks wildly about packing Bridget back to the Bahamas."

"Does he, indeed? He's apt to get a rush of blood to the brain sometimes," said Robert calmly. "This was after Bridget left, I suppose?"

"Yes. He demands to see her, but in this mood, I intend to see him first. Have you heard anything, Robert? I really am worried.

297

Bridget hasn't seemed herself lately, but I can't believe these wild accusations of Peter's."

"I've a good idea what it's all about. Don't worry, my dear. I want to see Bridget, and I'll come over. I'll probably catch her before she gets back, but if not, will you tell her to wait for me before seeing Uncle Peter. And don't take a refusal. Lock her in her study, if need be. She's not to face this without me."

"Very well, dear. Leave it to me. But Bridget isn't always the easiest girl to handle, so be as quick as you can. I shall be relieved to have you here. If we're going to have a family row, and I fear we are, I would like your judicial mind for support. Peter does get so heated. He always did, even as a small boy. I sometimes fear he will end up like Arthur, which would be very sad for poor Joyce. And I'm quite sure he has made a mistake about Bridget. She would never break up Felix's marriage. Peter has such an obsession about Susan, and it's possible that she's at the back of this."

It was so unusual for his grandmother to talk at such length on the telephone, an instrument with which she had never felt at home, that he knew she must be seriously disturbed. He uttered a few more reassuring words and rang off. Swearing under his breath, he shot off in his car to Melbridge. There was no sign of Bridget in the village, nor, dawdling along the heath, could he see any walkers. Under a bright sky with puffy white clouds moving fast in the wind, the heath stood out clearly in the bright light of early spring, the delicate tracery of silver birch trees reminding him of a Chinese drawing. He looked along the pathway which led to the pond, and remembered Bridget having a tug of war there with Boris, her hair bright in the sunshine, her green silk scarf fluttering in the wind.

A car hooted impatiently behind him, and he accelerated, irritably, his eyes alert for the figure of the girl he wished just then to throttle. He caught her halfway down the avenue which led from the village to Bredon Lodge. Leaning out of the car, he said in no gently tone:

"Hop in. I've got to talk to you."

"But I don't want to talk to you."

"Maybe not. But you're going to." He was out of the car now, holding the door open. As she hesitated, he gripped her arm and added, "If necessary, I'll throw you in."

He drove past Bredon Lodge, turned right at the end of the lane into a shady cul-de-sac and pulled up at the end, beside the boundary wall of a private school.

"Now we've not got much time, so we'll cut the cackle. Uncle Peter is waiting at Bredon Lodge for you now in a state of apoplexy, according to Grandma, having discovered that you have been paying his son-in-law's debts for him and jumping to the obvious conclusion that you're both as thick as thieves and that you are breaking up Felix's marriage."

"Oh no! How did he find out? Nobody knew."

"Except the man you paid. Bill Brent. He knew B. L. Armadale as the girl Felix used to run around with."

"But surely he wouldn't . . ."

"He let it out inadvertently when he was a bit lit up at a party at his golf club, with a crack about Felix's good luck in having a girl on the side who paid his debts instead of spending his money. I won't elaborate on what a bunch of men at a party would likely add by way of embroidery," concluded Robert wryly, and felt no compunction at the sight of her red cheeks.

"And someone repeated it to Uncle Peter?"

"He was there, standing at the bar nearby. Heard it all and tackled Brent, who pretended to be fuddled and incapable of understanding what he was talking about."

"Oh heavens!" exclaimed Bridget, shocked and distressed. "How do you know all this?"

"I met Brent in The Crown when I was having lunch today. He was suffering from a hang-over and an uneasy conscience. We know each other pretty well, and he told me about it, hoping I'd be able to suggest some way of lessening the damage. He only meant it as a joke, the silly ass. Now you see where your idiotic devotion to Felix has landed you. Or don't you mind? Do you want a show-down?"

"You know I don't. It was a business transaction, as I told you it was. Felix will pay me back. I did it to tide him over and give him a chance to save The Monitor."

"It still sounds like devotion to me. Anyway, we haven't time to argue that out now. The point is, Uncle Peter's out for your blood, and a first-class family scandal is about to explode. You'll get flayed, and a few others aren't going to feel so happy, either. The only way out I can think of is for me to spike Uncle Peter's guns and announce our engagement, and say I knew all about this loan. Whether we remain engaged after the sound and fury have died away is nobody's business but ours."

"Why should you do this, when you think I deserve what's coming?"

"Heaven knows! For some crazy reason, I feel responsible for you, and I can't throw you to the wolves."

"I don't want you to make sacrifices for me."

"Listen. You're not the only one I'm thinking about. This is going to raise a stink that will shock the old people, perhaps wreck Felix's marriage, and make your name mud, if we don't tone it down. What lies between you and me can be gone into later. This is merely a holding operation, and if you don't care about your reputation, think of others. Whatever cock-eyed, innocent version you may see as the truth, and I sometimes wonder if you'll ever acquire a shred of worldly wisdom, others will draw less pleasant conclusions. You may not mind what a pack of silly asses say about you in a club-house, but I mind, the grandparents would mind. We're

302

engaged. I knew about the loan. And leave the talking to me. Agreed?"

"Very well. It's no use saying I'm sorry I've landed you in for this, I suppose."

"Not much. And you'll be sorrier still when I've done with you and Felix. You'd better tell me as much about the financial aspect as you can. What debts were they? Where did The Monitor come in?"

She told him and added desperately:

"So you see, it was Felix's last chance of holding out against going into a business he'd loathe. He *is* a good journalist, Robert. You understand how important it is for a man to do the work of his choice, even if it is poorly paid."

"Yes, I know. Not many women would know, though," he added curiously, looking at her with an odd expression.

"I'd hate any man to give up work he liked just to keep me in comfort."

"When you take on responsibilities, you lose some of your freedom of action, Bridget. That's the price. You must take that into consideration before marrying. The trouble with Felix is that he's never wanted to pay any price. He wanted Susan, you, and a job which he liked but which wouldn't support a home

303

and a wife. He didn't want to pay any price when he married. He wanted, and still wants, the lot. And to trade on your foolish generosity and risk dragging you into this sort of muck is contemptible. He can go to the devil, for all I care, but you're involved, and something's got to be done. I ransacked Kit's room for this ring. I don't think anyone will recognise it. Mother left it to Kit with the idea of having the stones reset in a brooch. Put it on."

It was a little large, but looked well enough on her third finger. The ruby set between two diamonds glowed in a shaft of sunlight. This was an engagement with a difference, she thought unhappily, and far removed from the joyful occasion she had dreamed of in Nassau. Robert's attitude was stern, uncompromising. She feared that he saw this last act of folly as the final proof of a devotion to Felix which he would not and could not live with. And, in a way, she could not blame him. Where had she gone wrong? Perhaps it was a lack of worldly wisdom that had led her into such a compromising situation. She twisted the ring on her finger. A holding operation, Robert had said. And that he would stage-manage it so that the day was saved, she had no doubt. All the Rainwood family, of whatever age, had considerable respect for Robert, the eldest of his generation. With his calm assurance, his firm manner, his unquestionable air of competence and his success in his profession, Robert's counsel was listened to in the family; he counted. But they wouldn't come out of it unscathed, she thought; either of them.

"There's a call-box on the corner. I'll see if Felix is home. I don't know whether he knows what's happened yet—I rather think Uncle Peter is tackling you first—but we'd better put him in the picture so that we all tell the same story," said Robert grimly.

She waited in the car while he telephoned. He was not long, and asked no questions when he rejoined her with a cold anger in his eyes which chilled her. He made no comment on his conversation with Felix, merely saying, as he started the car:

"Leave the talking to me. I know Uncle Peter. Just follow my lead and try to look more like a happily engaged girl and less like a miserable sinner."

"All right. I'll do whatever you say."

"Then that'll be a record," said Robert unkindly, and swung the car back into the lane.

20

THE LONG GOODBYE

ROBERT took Bridget's arm in a firm hold as they went into the drawing-room, and she felt for one wild moment as though they were all taking part in one of Aunt Lucille's Christmas charades. Three pairs of eyes turned on them, and for a moment nobody spoke. Mirabel sat in her usual high-backed chair, her face calm but serious. Peter Rainwood was on the sofa, leaning forward with hands clasped, his face red and bad-tempered. Charles Rainwood stood by the window, hands clasped behind his back, looking as though he wished to disassociate himself from the rest. It was Robert who broke the silence, greeting them all easily and adding:

"I've only looked in for half an hour, Grandma, just to break the news. We think it's time we made our engagement known. We fixed it up when we were in Nassau, but thought we'd like a little time to get used to it ourselves before making it public."

"*Engaged?* You and Bridget?" said Peter incredulously.

"My dears, I'm delighted," said Mirabel. "And not altogether surprised. We wish you all the happiness in the world."

"Congratulations, Robert," said Charles, with obvious relief. "You've shown excellent judgment, if I may say so, but I hope you're not going to rob me of my assistant gardener too soon."

"I suppose you know what you're doing," said Peter ominously, and Robert turned a poker face to his uncle.

"I usually do. Why the pessimistic note?"

"Why? I'll tell you, though I thought you had a good idea of what's been in the wind. Bridget has never stopped running after Felix, and now she's managed to get their names linked in a most unsavoury fashion. It's common talk in Oakdene."

"Do enlighten us," said Robert calmly, drawing a chair forward for Bridget and taking up his favourite stance in front of the fireplace as he took out his pipe.

"You know yourself all the talk there was soon after Sue married Felix. She was under

308

no illusions about Bridget, I can tell you, but she was ready to smile at it, thinking that Bridget would soon tire of running after a man who was happily married."

"Really, Peter, I object to this," said Charles sternly. "You're behaving like an old woman, stirring up trouble."

"Felix and I were old friends, Uncle Peter," said Bridget quietly. "There has never been anything more than friendship between us, and I've seen hardly anything of him since I left The Monitor."

"You've tried to bribe your way back by paying his debts, giving him money."

"Bridget agreed to offer Felix a loan, after consulting me, as a bridging operation while he negotiated an amalgamation with another magazine. Nothing sinister in that, Uncle Peter, surely," said Robert coldly.

"You knew about it?"

"Of course."

"Then you're less intelligent than I thought, or you'd have stopped it."

"I don't say I altogether approved. I pointed out to Bridget the risk of losing her money, or at least of having to wait a long time for it, since I have no great opinion of Felix Parvey's business capacity, but they had known each other from childhood and it was hard for her to refuse Felix's appeal for help, particularly as she had some regard for The Monitor herself and would hate to see it go under."

"Well, of course, if you knew about it," grumbled Peter. "But I can't understand you allowing her to do it. Do you know what I overheard in our club-house bar last night?"

"Tell us," said Robert, lighting his pipe.

"I don't see any point in repeating such gossip," said Charles stiffly. "Bad taste, and not fit for Bridget's ears, anyway. I object."

"Robert has a right to know what people are saying about the girl he's engaged to," said Peter obstinately, and repeated the story.

"Bill Brent's an ass, but a decent enough chap," said Robert mildly. "He must have been well under the influence to play to the gallery like that. I'll have a word with him, but I shouldn't get hot and bothered about stories served up at a stag party. I'll see that Bill makes amends as far as he can, but I feel that the less said, the better."

"You mean to say you don't mind?"

"Of course I mind, but since the conclusions they drew were false, I don't intend to lose any sleep over it, or embark on an action for slander. I advise you to forget it, Uncle Peter. It would only distress Susan to hear about it, though you might care to tell Felix that Bridget won't come to his aid any more and she'd rather not be involved in any way again. Isn't that so, dear?"

"Yes," said Bridget. "I'm sorry for what happened at your club, Uncle Peter, but I can't help it if people have low minds."

"It seems to me that you want to watch your step more carefully, young woman. Now that you're engaged, perhaps you'll consider Robert's feelings. If you'll kindly tell me the amount of the loan, I'll give you a cheque now."

Bridget told him and he made out the cheque there and then, whipping it out of his cheque book and handing it to her with an expression of disgust.

"I should have thought you would have had more pride than to try to buy your way back into Felix's life. I only hope Robert won't repent of his choice."

"Really, Peter," broke in his mother, exasperated as she saw Bridget wince and turn white, "you really must mind your own business and leave Robert to mind his. You come here with all sorts of wild accusations

311

against Bridget which, if they're spread around, could do untold harm, and now you're acting like the old witches in Macbeth, prophesying doom. You're so melodramatic. You makes everything sound like a sensational Sunday newspaper story. You manufacture trouble."

"I, manufacture trouble for my own daughter, when I'm only concerned with her happiness?"

"Then leave those two children alone, to sort out their own marriage."

"I bitterly regret the day I let my daughter marry Parvey. But I'll have a talk to that young man. You can be sure of that. I still think Bridget's most to blame. Now, perhaps, he'll listen to me."

"Power has gone to your head and is making you an egomaniac, Peter," said Mirabel crisply. "If you interfere in Susan's marriage, you'll ruin their chances of happiness. Any man would resent his father-in-law dictating to him. Felix married Susan, not you."

"Well, I'm not going to stay here and be lectured. Any lecturing to be done should be aimed at Owen's stepdaughter," said Peter spitefully. "You've always had a blind spot where she's concerned. Heaven knows why."

"Shall we all stay calm," said Robert, "and agree that the less said about the knowing remarks of some chaps who'd been celebrating, the better? They were only trying to appear gay sparks, men of the world, for a brief interval before returning to their sober, respectable middle-class lives. A pity to take it too seriously and make unnecessary trouble."

"Of course," said Charles Rainwood. "Drink seems to have a very foolish, inflating effect on some men. Never had that effect on me. Only gave me a headache and a feeling of deep pessimism. Scarcely touch it now."

"That's all very well," began Peter, and how long he would have continued in this strain was a matter of conjecture, for at that moment Arthur Rainwood erupted into the room.

"What damned fool left his car just inside the gate, blocking the drive?" he demanded, glaring at them.

"Are you referring to my car?" asked Peter stiffly.

"A black Jaguar. You change cars so often, I never know how high up the ladder you've got."

"I was forced to leave it there because some tradesman had parked his van across the drive, for some obscure reason."

"You should have asked him to straighten up, then. Parking just inside the gate like that. Quite invisible from the road, with the high hedges. Asking for trouble. Sorry about the damage, Peter, but it's your own fault."

"Damage? What damage?" demanded Peter, his voice moving a tone higher.

Robert caught Bridget's eye, and lifted his eyebrows heavenwards, his long mouth twitching at the corners. It was the first human expression she had seen on his face that day, and it dispelled a little of the chill in her heart.

"The rear light and a bit of a dent in the wing."

"*What*? I suppose you roared into the drive in your usual lunatic fashion. People of your age shouldn't be allowed to drive. How much damage are you going to be allowed to do before you're disqualified?"

"Nothing wrong with my driving."

"You drive like a reckless lunatic. It's a miracle that you've escaped with your skin intact for so long."

"I'm the aggrieved party, not you. My

314

front light is smashed and the front wing bent, but I'm not one to make a fuss about a few scratches."

"I doubt whether they'd notice on that old wreck of yours. How it ever passes the road test, I'll never know. You probably don't bother to have it tested. Just take a chance."

"I don't regard my car as a status symbol," said Arthur Rainwood, a wicked light in his eye, his anger descending as his nephew's rose.

"Well," said Mirabel firmly, "you'd better go and see just what has happened, Peter, and continue your wrangling outside."

They went, still arguing, and Charles uttered a sigh of relief.

"What a to-do! I really don't know where Peter gets his fussy ways, Mirabel. Don't be upset over his accusations, Bridget. You acted for the best, I'm sure. I'd like to give those oafs at that party a piece of my mind. Bandying words about like that, damaging innocent girls. Not the conduct of gentlemen, but then I suppose I'm old-fashioned even to use the word."

"I think you are, dear," said his wife.

"Well, I must say I'm shocked that a son of mine should repeat such gossip to a young girl like Bridget, and even appear to believe it."

"I was foolish, I suppose, to lend Felix the money," said Bridget. "I didn't foresee this kind of interpretation."

"Why should you? Just forget it, my dear. I'm going out in the garden to repair the pergola. Need some fresh air after all this. Are you taking Bridget off with you this afternoon, Robert?"

"Only for half an hour. We've a few things to discuss. After that, I've got to get back and pack a case for the night train to Exeter. I've some business in the west country on Monday, and I want to look Kit up tomorrow. She hasn't been well. A dose of food poisoning. Better now, but she sounded a bit subdued on the telephone."

"Well, I'm sorry the atmosphere has been so bleak for the announcement of your engagement, my dears," said Mirabel, "but we must have a proper celebration in the near future. A family party."

"We're a bit allergic to family congratulations at the moment, Grandma," said Robert. "I think we'd both prefer you to spread the news for us and leave the family party for another occasion. I'm not exactly a party man."

Mirabel looked at them thoughtfully, then said:

"As you wish, Robert. Are you sure you won't stay for tea?"

"Quite sure, thanks."

"Then I'll say goodbye, dear, and go and see what your grandfather proposes to do with the pergola. I don't myself think it's worth repairing. Give my love to Christine."

When they were alone, Robert said:

"Let's go up to your study. Uncle Peter may bounce back at any moment and I've seen enough of him for one day."

In her study, he went to the window and stood staring out, his hands behind his back, while Bridget looked at him helplessly. Their feelings had been shredded, and she felt that any words now would be useless. He came back to the desk and sat on a corner of it, picking up the glass paper-weight and considering it in a preoccupied way before replacing it with deliberate care.

"Well, Bridget, it wasn't exactly pretty, was it?"

"No. I've said I'm sorry for landing you in this situation."

"That's not the point, is it? That money represented the major part of what remained of the legacy from your stepfather, I suppose."

"Yes. Practically all I had left. I'd spent a good deal, fitting myself out for Nassau and subsidising myself before that. The advance payment for my part of the Corrie and Birch book didn't go far, but it took all my time and I couldn't earn anything from freelancing."

"So you beggared yourself for him. A good thing Uncle Peter paid you back today," he said dryly.

She took two letters out of her desk and handed them to him.

"I'd like you to read these. The letter Felix wrote me as soon as I arrived back from Nassau, and his reply to the one I wrote asking him to let me tell you about it."

He read them and handed them back, saying:

"Felix's opinion of me seems to be about as low as mine of him."

"He doesn't know you, and you don't know him."

"I know enough about him. He nearly broke your heart by throwing you over, he played on your friendship to make use of you and borrow money from you, and then has the nerve to admit that gossip that harms your reputation would be preferable to letting his own shaky financial state be known. What sort of a man is that?"

"Kind, but weak," she said steadily.

"Anyway, he's right about one thing. When you told me that it was a business matter you met to discuss, I should have believed you. I'm sorry. It was such a cracking jolt after Nassau that I saw red. I know you're not dishonest. But sometimes I wonder if you know yourself."

"I do. You're mistaking my stepfather's version of me for what I am. You always have. He held up a mirror that showed my mother and told you it was me. And you believed him."

"With all the evidence to prove him right," said Robert savagely. "Do you think I haven't remembered time and time again your face at Felix's wedding; your despair that night I took you home after Felix and Susan had caught you at Grandma's. You weren't acting, Bridget. You were grief-stricken. And you told me yourself that you couldn't put him out of your heart. He'd been there too long."

"And at the party for Kit and Nicholas's birthday only four months later, I felt I'd got

319

over it, and I began to realise that there was another world besides the narrow little one I'd been living in."

"Yes, you were happy that night."

"You kissed me goodnight."

Her voice was muffled. She was standing with her back to him, her hand moving over the conch shell on the book-case where once Felix's photograph had stood. He crossed the room and turned her to him, ignoring the tears in her eyes.

"Then why, in heaven's name, have you let yourself be involved with him so often since, when you knew how Susan felt, how gossip had already been aroused? And then to answer his appeal with all the money you had, when you knew how I felt."

"I can see now that it was foolish, Robert. But none of it was wrong. The only wrong thing about it has been the world's interpretation. Can I be blamed for that?"

"Knowing the world, yes. And if you don't know it at your age, you ought to. The interpretation the world made was all too likely, and you must have known what damage it could do. I warned you enough times."

"Yes. But I didn't willingly get involved with Felix again, Robert. I wasn't interested.

He wasn't in my mind, once your friendship began to count. But he sought me out, he appealed to me for old times' sake. Yes, I know that sounds corny, but I wonder if you realise what my life was like after my mother died. It was solitary, cut off from all young people by my stepfather's cold unsociability, and I was subjected all the time to cutting criticism, made to feel unwanted and despised. I was too young to realise that my stepfather was venting on me his hatred of my father and his failure with my mother. I just accepted it as my environment, and never thought I'd escape from it. I never even challenged it. Children don't, somehow. They have a kind of stoicism. So you can imagine what Felix's friendship meant to me. We became friends when I was thirteen years old. He was fifteen. We walked to school together and came home together. It grew from that. And never, in all those years, did he fail in kindness to me. When he made that appeal, I couldn't refuse. It seemed little enough by way of repayment for making all those years of childhood and girlhood tolerable, even happy when we were together. It's the past. Over and done with. It has nothing to do with my life now. But gratitude for the past—that's something I couldn't and shouldn't forget. Can't you understand how it was, Robert, and believe that I've said goodbye to the past? Won't you, too?"

"It's been a long goodbye, my love," he said gently.

"I know. Too long, but not by my wish."

"Only by too soft and unworldly a heart. You know, if I hadn't cared so much, it wouldn't have seemed so important. I couldn't bear to make the sort of hash your stepfather made, but I'm jealous and possessive. I could hurt you. I discovered that about myself recently, and didn't feel proud of it."

"The only way you could hurt me would be by not loving me. But if you love me, I expect that to mean that you trust me. Felix and Susan will still be in the family circle. If there is always to be this suspicion like a canker, then perhaps it would be better for us to part, though I can't bear the thought of it. I should have to go right away. Back to Nassau, perhaps. I was happy there. And live on my dreams, as Mother did, but they'd be of you, Robert."

"Unworldly again. You'd be snapped up by some rich American. Do you think I'm going to risk that? I know what blue lagoons and white sand do to you."

She tried to smile, but it was a very quavery effort, and he drew her into his arms.

"All right, my dear. Perhaps it needed this kind of blow-up to sort ourselves out. I've apologised for some of the things I said, and I think this afternoon you really did finish saying that long goodbye to Felix. Shall we go on from there, and try to make a go of it?"

"Yes, please."

"Well, dry your eyes, or Grandma will think I've been beating you. I wish to goodness I hadn't arranged this west-country trip, but I'll have to go."

"When will you be back?"

"Tuesday morning. I must look in at the office for a couple of hours, but how about meeting me for lunch, and then buying a ring?"

"We'll never get one to look like this."

"Well, I don't think anybody took much notice of it in all the furore this afternoon, but if they did, we can always say you didn't like it, after all, and we changed it. Then, perhaps, we'll stay in town and go to a show, or else come home and drive out to that little inn at Fernleigh for dinner. You said once that you'd never been there and liked the look of it."

"The one by the lake, you mean?"

"Yes."

"That would be lovely." She clutched him. "But I wish you weren't going away. You won't start thinking about Felix and having doubts again, will you? Today, we really have buried the past, haven't we?"

"Yes. And I must say, it had a thumping funeral. I'll never forget Uncle Peter's face when Great-Uncle Arthur told him he'd run into his brand-new Jag. Not Uncle Peter's day. And then dear old Grandpa going all quaint and old-fashioned on us. I almost expected him to challenge Bill Brent and Uncle Peter to a duel with pistols at dawn tomorrow. We shan't forget the day we got engaged."

"Well, you may smile, but Grandpa's not the only one with a sense of chivalry. You could so easily have said, 'Serve the wretched girl right', and have left me to face the storm."

"I seem to remember talking a lot of nonsense about a moment of choice, but I don't think I ever had any choice of not being involved with you right up to my neck ever since that day when you looked as desperate as a trapped hare and said 'Help me'. Remember?"

"Yes."

"Not that you kept up that submissive air for long. It was splendid bait for my bossy instincts, though. Ever since, I've been irrevocably committed, though perhaps I didn't finally admit it to myself until I heard Bill Brent's tale. And then I knew all right. And felt sorry for your stepfather."

"And you know now that there's no parallel."

His eyes met hers and he said quietly:

"I know now."

If Bridget still had any doubts about whether the ghost of Felix and the past had been finally laid, they were removed on the following Tuesday, when Robert's confident happiness was unmistakable, and her own joy bubbled up in response.

She went back to Bredon Lodge to change for the evening, and at Robert's request, wore the blue chiffon dress she had worn in Nassau. On her wrist was the bracelet he had given her there, and on her third finger, a diamond and ruby engagement ring he had bought her that day, a much more delicate ring than his mother's but she had wanted the same warm glow of rubies.

When he called for her, she led him up to her study.

"I wanted to show you this before I destroy it. From Felix."

"My dear, you don't have to show me."

"I know. But I want you to read it. The last words on the matter."

He read it with one arm round her shoulders.

Dear Biddy,

Sorry about the row my father-in-law caused. He is a man of little sensibility. I gather Robert saved the day for you.

For me, it's lost. The deal with Hugh Downing fell through, anyway. He may have heard rumours. I have agreed to join my father-in-law's firm, at a princely salary, with a directorship as soon as I've learned the business. I wouldn't have agreed, but Sue is going to have a baby in the autumn, and that clinched it. Now that the decision is taken, it's a relief in a dull sort of way. I'm so tired of always being under pressure.

Sue and I are going to make a fresh start.

Having a child will help, perhaps. There is talk of our moving to London. My father-in-law is fed up with the travelling, and is looking at property in the Kensington area with a view to suiting himself and finding something for us, too, in the same vicinity. I don't mind much one way or the other, but a London home will be a more convenient proposition now that I'm going to be working there.

There's not much more to say, except thank you for everything. You know how I feel. There's nothing to be done about that. I hope you and Robert will be very happy. He doesn't deserve his good luck, but I think he'll look after you.

I shall always look on our friendship as one of the best things that ever happened to me. I hope you will always think kindly of it, too.

Yours ever,
Felix

"Well, well," said Robert. "Now that I'm not jealous of him, I can feel sorry for him."

"Yes." She tore up the letter and threw the pieces into the waste-paper basket. "The end of a chapter. Let's start the new one."

"It promises well, don't you think?" asked Robert, smiling.

"Very well," she said, and slid her hand under his arm as they went downstairs.

Mirabel Rainwood stood at the window of the drawing-room and looked out at the darkening garden. The sun had set and the first stars were visible in a deep blue sky. Beneath the trees, the daffodils swayed in the breeze, pale and heartbreakingly lovely in the dusk. At the far end of the lawn, the almond tree, in full bloom, stood like a pale, ethereal ghost. All day the rooks had been noisily busy about their nests at the top of the ash trees, but now they had fallen silent and the last solitary rook was winging its way across the garden to the roost. She was glad they had returned to make their rookery in the ash trees again. Noisy, clumsy, comical birds, their cawing was a pleasant, companionable sound in the garden. Another spring already. If only one could put a brake on the fastly spinning seasons.

She turned away from the garden with a little sigh for the transience of life, and switched on the lamp by her bureau. Drawing out her diary, she wrote:

Almost a year since Susan married Felix Parvey, and now Bridget and Robert are engaged and intend to be married this summer. I am very happy indeed that my dear Robert has at last chosen to marry. I began to fear he was set for a bachelor's life. And I could wish him no happier choice than Bridget, who has a loving heart and will repay his devotion tenfold.

I was a little uneasy when they announced it last Saturday. Peter was all set on stirring up that old gossip about Bridget and Felix, and I had the impression that Robert was being quixotic. Bridget looked like a ghost, and was wearing that pretty ring which Robert's mother inherited from her mother. I remember Grace showing it to me only a few weeks before the accident.

This evening, Robert has taken Bridget out to dinner and the picture was entirely changed. Nobody can light up quite like Bridget when she is happy. She looked really radiant tonight, and wore a new engagement ring which I duly admired without remarking on the quick change. Robert is not quixotic by nature. He is a very rational man. He must be very much in love with Bridget. They obviously had no doubts at all tonight, so I conclude that Felix has been rubbed out in the wash.

It occurred to me on Saturday, not for the first time, how much I have been helped throughout my life by Charles's simple goodness. His attitude to Peter was typical. How much less difficult life is when one is so certain of one's values.

Robert thinks that this diary would be a valuable source of information for a social historian of the future, but I doubt it. To be that, I would have to dwell more on the fixtures and fittings and everyday little happenings of my life rather than indulge myself in reflections on human nature, but I have always found people more interesting than fixtures and fittings and daily routine, and I doubt whether anybody outside the family would find these diaries particularly interesting. After all, except to ourselves, we are a very ordinary family.

THE END

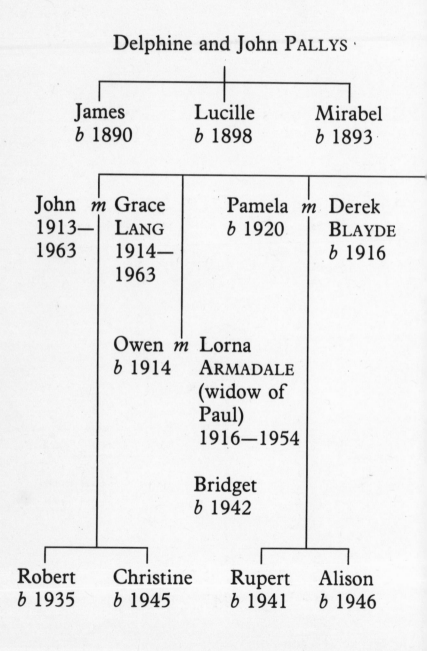

Delphine and John PALLYS

James
b 1890

Lucille
b 1898

Mirabel
b 1893

John *m* Grace
1913— LANG
1963   1914—
       1963

Pamela *m* Derek
b 1920   BLAYDE
         b 1916

Owen *m* Lorna
b 1914   ARMADALE
         (widow of
         Paul)
         1916—1954

         Bridget
         b 1942

Robert
b 1935

Christine
b 1945

Rupert
b 1941

Alison
b 1946